# THE DEVIL AND THE AWESOME FOUR

# BOOK 1
# RISE OF THE FOUR

## DAMON RAVENBLOOD

RAVENBLOOD PRESS

# CONTENTS

# DEDICATIONS

This book is dedicated to the following:
Mom, Dad, Alan, Lisa, Noel, Jennifer, Anton, Ben, Kate,
Paudie, Hayley, and Mike.
To my wife Caroline and my Step Kids
For all my aunts, uncles, cousins and friends, too numerous
to mention individually, but you know who you are.
Eliza Knight, whose ideas and assistance with this book are
greatly appreciated.

# INTRODUCTION

When Ben Connors, Roger Ryan, Jackie Anderson, and Sarah Thomas met, they got more than they bargained for. From the word go, hell was hot on their trail, casting them into a world where the supernatural and paranormal reign supreme. Fate had brought them together for a reason, to fight the forces of evil and the dominions of hell. They were four young people with uncomplicated lives, until evil reared its ugly head forcing them to take action and go to battle, with a whole load of trouble to follow.

The Devil himself becomes involved and tries his best to destroy our heroes, sending maniacs, demons and a whole lot more to destroy them, before his ultimate goal can be accomplished. When the four met, they inadvertently set in motion the countdown to Armageddon and now is Satan's chance to return and wreak havoc upon humanity, the only thing standing in his way are the Awesome four and he will stop at nothing to eradicate them. From his chainsaw wielding terror named Harry Gordon, who gives up his soul to become an immortal killing machine that leaves bodies strewn in his wake and as he encounters the four heroes, blood is going to fly. Satan even tricks the four into travelling to the future under the pretence that they are protecting the new Messiah. When Stephanie the vampire queen comes to town, all hell breaks loose and poor Ben becomes a tortured man, and when something strange happens to his beloved Jackie things get a little confusing. As we catch up with Ben and Roger, we find them standing at Dublin airport ready to embark on a new life of sun, sea, and happiness. If only that were true. Let's join them now and follow their journey from ordinary saps to American Heroes.

# THE BEGINNING

B en Connors and Roger Ryan are close friends and have been for over ten years. Ben is a 26-year-old, factory worker at a steel fabricating firm. Roger is 27 and works in an electronics enterprise specialized in assembling computers for a small firm. They are both exhausted and depressed by the thought of the countless years laid out before them, so they decided, to leave their present lives far behind them. They've had this planned for two years, but the lack of funds held them off, until now. This was their golden opportunity to break free from the chains that have held them back for so long and Los Angeles California was their chosen destination. They arrived at the airport on the big day and found the lobby, packed to capacity with people rushing to their right terminals or arguing with staff about over booked flights or plane tickets that were not issued on time. It was pandemonium. Not letting the chaos deter them,they handed the clerk their passports, then she handed them the tickets to their new lives.

"Your tickets gentlemen,"

She said with a smile, her bleached white teeth sparkling in the overhead fluorescent light.

"Thank you." replied Ben with a flirty smile, wider than the clerks.

"Will you come on?" Roger said, pulling Ben by the arm leading him away.

Ben took one last look out the lobby window at the place, which he hoped to never return.

"Goodbye and good riddance to this depressing place. All of our lives, we have been pretty much trapped here with a bleak outlook ahead and no future, now it's time to leave and never look back.

After two hours waiting, the last call for flight 756 Los Angeles came through the intercom, the invitation the guys had been waiting to hear. "This is going to be great. Sun, sea, booze, and women, what more could a guy want?" Roger said with a little laugh as they slung their backpacks over their shoulders and proceeded to terminal 2.

As they walked up the gangway, a hostess asked them for their tickets.

Then they walked down the aisle placing their backpacks in the overhead luggage compartments before taking their seats and fastening their seat belts.

The engines roared as the plane taxied into position.

With final checks completed, the pilots received the go ahead from the control tower. The Boeing rocketed down the runway slowly lifting off. The guys felt their ears pop becoming a little queasy.

Six hours later the tires of the landing gear screeched along the tarmac, as the plane landed in California.

"L.A. here we are!" they both said as they disembarked.

They walked into the terminal and proceeded through customs where the officers examined their cases, and passports, and once they were satisfied with Roger and Ben, stamped and approved their visas, they then walked outside, hailed a taxi and asked to be taken to the nearest Motel.

They drove for what seemed like forever, with the driver ranting on about everything from politics and religion to just downright old bullshit. Then, the taxi stopped outside what looked like a rundown sleazy joint, they hopped out and handed him twenty dollars each. The cabbie drove off, while the driver yelled out his window "Welcome to Los Angeles", honked his horn and disappeared into the distance. They walked into the motel, down the damp ridden cockroach infested hallway, and knocked on door number one. The landlord opened it. He was in his late forties heavy set, greasy balding head, wearing a string vest that looked as if he wore it for the past ten years without washing it, a cigarette hung from the corner of his mouth, a can of Budweiser in his left hand, his trousers were unbuttoned his big beer belly hanging over the waist line and he looked like he needed at least four showers just to remove the surface grime. The smell of stale smoke and sweat almost made their eyes water.

"Yeah, what do ya want?" He barked with his eyes firmly fixed on the guys.

"Ah, Sorry to have bothered you" Ben said as he and Roger backed away from the man and hurried down through the damp ridden corridor with the landlord hurling insults at them.

They strolled on for about ten minutes before they came across another motel. Ben winked at Roger and smiled as they walked down the corridor to the landlord's apartment and knocked. Not sure what to expect, they held their breath as someone unlocked a security chain from the other side. A man appeared in the doorway. He was in his mid-fifties, remarkably well dressed and pleasant.

"Can I help you guys?" He asked in a Gentle, friendly tone.

"Yes, you can," Roger said, putting down his bags to catch his breath, "we need a room for a few nights nothing too big and hopefully not too expensive."

"I think I can help you there just give me a second." The man went back inside. A few moments later, he came out with a huge bunch of keys.

"Follow me." He led the way down the corridor. The guys couldn't believe it, they were expecting a real kip, but this was great. The walls were painted a lime green colour with paintings of the ocean, a forest, a lighthouse, to name a few, and the floors were pinewood and well kept. They walked down the corridor, until they came to a stop outside door 32, the landlord then opened the door. The room was nice enough, but they didn't care about stuff like that as long as they had a place to crash for a few nights. "How much do you charge a night?" Roger asked half expecting it to be pricey.

"It will be fifty a night per person with two nights deposit up front." The man spun the bunch of keys round his index finger.

"We'll take it." Ben had an exhausted look in his eyes. The man handed them their keys.

"Enjoy your stay." He said closing the door behind him.

"Let's try to get some sleep, then get ready to hit the town," Ben said, and threw himself on the couch, Roger lay on one of the beds.

After about four hours of sleep, they awoke:

"I'm just going to grab a quick shower Ben," Roger walked to the bathroom locking the door behind him. Ben looked in his travel mirror and noticed he had about a day's growth of stubble.

"Man, this won't do at all. I'll have a shave when Rodge gets out," and just as he had the last word spoken the door unlocked and Roger appeared.

"I'm going to have a shave and a quick shower. Won't be long," he said entering the bathroom. Fifteen minutes later they were dressed up and ready to party. Smelling of Old Spice aftershave and Lynx Body Spray.

They went out for a few drinks, which lasted two hours, before they came upon a nightclub called, "Aces High". The place was packed, and people were being turned away, as they reached the doors the doormen stopped them explaining that the place was almost full, Ben was quick to reply.

"Almost full doesn't mean completely full now does it. Come on man, we've travelled a long way, so how's about cutting us some slack," he smiled at the Bouncer who pondered for a moment before his supervisor winked and nodded.

He removed the security rope stepping aside letting them enter.

"Thanks man we appreciate it," Ben said with a nod and a grin. Roger patted him on the shoulder

"Let's grab a beer and go mingle," he pointed to the bar. Up at the bar, things were a little crowded and they accidentally bumped into two women, spilling some of their drinks but they were the ones who apologized.

"Apologize for what? It was us that bumped into you," Roger said with a smile. The girls laughed and introduced themselves.

"I'm Jackie and this mad one here is Sarah," One of them said. She was twenty-two-years-old, five foot nine, with long, straight black hair, lightly tanned skin and dark blue eyes. In other words, drop dead gorgeous.

"I'm Ben," he said a little shyly, "and this is Roger." They all shook hands and chatted until they got to the bar. The girls called for beers as did the guys who paid for the lot. After two more drinks, they realized that they were getting to like each other more and more, so much, so that Ben kissed Jackie. Just as, their lips parted, the lovers' songs played.

"Want to dance?" Jackie stood up from the table holding out her hand

He looked at Roger, "She's asking me to dance? That would normally be my line. Beaten at my own game," he said with a smile, took her hand, and led her to the dance floor.

They were kissing like crazy when someone tapped Ben on the shoulder. He looked around; there were Roger and Sarah beside them with Roger grinning like a Cheshire cat. The lover's songs finished, and they returned to their seats.

"I'm tired," Sarah, said stretching, and yawning, her breasts sticking out through her tight top.

"Want to go home?" Jackie added, laying on the hint.

"You bet I do," Ben said reading her body language. She laughed as she and Sarah went to the cloakroom to collect their coats.

"God those two made our night, didn't they?" Sarah said with a fantasizing look in her eyes.

"They sure have. God, I'm so glad we came out," Jackie replied, biting her bottom lip.

They got their coats and went back only to find the two guys sprawled across their seats almost asleep. "Wake up," Sarah yelled over the loud music.

The guys jolted awake and got to their feet, and Ben asked

"Are we going back to your place or ours?"

They walked out into the streets arm in arm right passed the guy's motel. They walked about half a mile until Jackie said. "Well, this is our stop I'll call you later, Sarah okay," She led Ben up to her front door.

Roger and Sarah walked for another five minutes before arriving at her house.

Ben and Jackie were getting hot and heavy on her couch. He unzipped her red dress and removed her bra. Her large breasts spilled down her chest; their size amazed him. She took off his shirt and unbuttoned his jeans, she stood and slinked her way out of her dress and climbed back on top of him, spreading her legs so her crotch rested on his lap. She kissed his chest working her way up to his lips. He caressed her breasts while she kissed his neck. Passion and lust got the better of them, and they had hot passionate sex.

Jackie was lost in the heat of passion as she yelled with pleasure and panted.

"That was fucking Awesome," she said through her rapid breathing.

After another round of love making, Ben got dressed and was heading out the door when Jackie pulled him back slipping him a piece of paper on which was her number. She kissed him again, went back inside and gently closed the door. Ben was on cloud nine walking out the gate when Roger came towards him.

"Well?" Roger asked, smiling.

"Well, what?" came the reply and huge grin.

"How did you get on?" Roger asked.

"It was fantastic. I've never had anything that even comes close to that in my life," he said with a laugh of victory.

"I'm meeting Jackie tomorrow are you going to meet Sarah?" Ben asked as they walked.

"Yes, I'm meeting her at twelve at the mall," Roger placed his cold hands in his pockets

"Isn't that great that's the time I'm to meet Jackie at the mall too" Ben lit up a smoke.

They got back to their motel and celebrated their good fortune with a few beers.

"I was just thinking Roger, instead of meeting them at the mall, why don't we meet them at Jackie's," He finished his beer, fumbled around in his jeans pocket for the scrap of paper Jackie gave to him before he left with her number on it. He picked up the phone and dialled. He waited for the ring but it went straight to her answering machine instead. He left a brief voice mail and tried to place the receiver back in the cradle but fell forward off the chair and lay on the floor. And there he slept until the next morning.

It was just gone ten, when Ben woke up to a blaring siren as a fire truck screamed past the motel. He held his head with both hands as a terrible headache crept across his brow.

"*Oh Christ! Never again will I drink that much,*" He whispered to himself as Roger rose from his drunken slumber.

It was now 10.45, time to take a shower then join the girls later.

They left the motel; the sun was beating down on them. They made a quick stop to buy cold sodas and continued on their way, sweat dripping from their brows. "God, I'm melting," Roger said, taking a sip of his now, warm cola.

"I know it's blistering," Ben replied, wiping the sweat from his forehead.

They arrived at Jackie's right on time, and the girls were waiting for them

"Well, hello again" Jackie said coming to the front door when she saw the guys walking up the pathway

"So, where do we go now?" Ben asked giving her a peck on the cheek.

"We were thinking about the old Lummis castle, it's a beautiful day so we may as well walk. Will you take this Ben?" Jackie asked with a smile, handing him a picnic basket.

All four of them walked for about two miles, before the castle came into view, it was enormous and in superb condition for a 900-year-old landmark. They looked around until they came to its courtyard. They saw an open door that led into what used to be a secret escape tunnel.

Ben left the basket behind a pillar, and they went to explore.

They followed the spiralling staircase to the bottom into a cavern. On the walls, lit torches cast their dim light into the shadows. Ben kissed Jackie without warning. She giggled and kissed him back. Their lips parted.

"Did you hear something?" She said, startled, glancing around her, eyes wide with shock. "I heard nothing?" He said, looking around listening attentively, and this time he did hear something, very faint but it sounded like some kind of chanting.

Another chorus of voices echoed from deep within the cavern.

"Let's follow it and see what happens?" Jackie said as they proceeded toward an open door at the back of the cavern.

They dashed inside and hid behind a stone pillar. At least 50 people with black cloaks and hoods stood in a pentagram pattern.

"Who are they?" Sarah whispered as she clung to Roger looking at them.

"They're Satanists. It looks like someone's about to be sacrificed." Ben pointed as a young man was brought forward from the shadows screaming and fighting as he was dragged before the high priest.

They stripped him and painted an inverted cross upon his chest in pig's blood that dripped down his body in narrow rivulets. He was forced to lie down in the middle of a painted pentagram on the floor, four disciples held his arms and legs as he struggled and yelled for help. The high priest knelt behind his head, reading a passage from an ancient book then raised a dagger aloft praying in Latin, he lowered the blade, grabbed the terrified young man by the hair raising his head from the floor, his eyes opened wide in terror as he felt the cold blade across his throat. The man gagged as his blood poured from gaping slit across his throat flowing across the floor, the pentagram began to glow a sinister luminous green, the disciples steeped back forming a circle. A gateway had been opened; the dead man's body sank into the black hole that had now appeared in the middle of the floor, followed by a terrible blood curdling roar that echoed from the giant hole, a colossal hand appeared, then another. A monstrous beast was emerging and the high priest was panicking, turning pages in a rush trying to stop what he had started, but it was too late. The Cyclopean demon now stood menacingly before them staring at the terrified cult.

The worshippers were chanting something in a language long dead to this world. The demon stood at least ten feet tall, with a single piercing yellow eye in the centre of its forehead, razor-sharp claws, and teeth. It roared and with one slash of its claws sent a man's head rolling across the ground the body still standing, nerves firing making it dance and tremble, blood gushing everywhere. Jackie clasped her hand across her mouth to stop herself from screaming as the demon went berserk. The other worshippers panicked and ran. Screams of terror and suffering echoed through the caverns as the slaughter continued. Dismembered limbs, blood, and shredded robes were all that remained of fifty people. The high priest was trying to open the latch on the steel gate, pulling and pushing but to no avail. He grabbed the bars shaking the gate and kicking it when he heard heavy breathing behind him. He turned pale as he slowly turned to face the thing he had let loose. The beast reached out a massive hand seizing its summoner by the throat. The man coughed and gagged as the fingers tightened around his neck. He was lifted high into the air then felt the demons other hand seize his legs. With a mighty roar the beast ripped the man in two and a shower of blood splashed across the floor covering its feet. The head of the severed torsos mouth was opening and closing as if trying to mutely curse this bastard monster, when it fell still eyes glassy and vacant, the spinal column trembled and pulsated as the life ebbed away. The demon roared again flinging the horrid remains each side of the room.

Suddenly, it turned its attention to where Ben, Jackie, Sarah, and Roger were hiding. Moving like lightning, it was upon them. Pointed teeth lined its vicious jaws and evil eye sent shivers down their spines. It swung its claws at Roger who ducked and ran to Ben.

"How the hell do we stop this thing?" He screamed over the howling shriek of the wind emanating from the vortex.

"I don't know Rodge, if it came from that gateway then maybe it must go back through it, I don't know, but we have to try and stop it somehow before it gets out." Ben yelled, as Jackie grabbed him by the arm

"How the hell do we stop it, Ben? You just saw what it done to those clowns; what chance do the four of us have against it?" She yelled, as the beast went on the attack again.

They ran deeper into the cavern, down stony corridors with the creature's grunts and growls echoing behind them. They stopped to catch their breath, placing their hands on their knees panting and gasping. Jackie happened to cast her eyes over Ben's shoulder and spied a solid oak door.

"Ben, look behind you," he jumped thinking the demon was about to grab him, as he turned, he saw the door. Placing his shoulder against it he pushed with all his might but it didn't budge. The others came to help and as they pushed, the door slowly gave way, painfully slow. A guttural roar sent shivers down their spines as the demon's shadow appeared upon the wall illuminated by the burning glow of a torch.

"One more big push, come on," Ben yelled and the door suddenly gave way and they ended up in a heap on the ground. They quickly regained their feet and pushed the door shut, it creaked and squeaked until it finally latched. They found themselves in total darkness. Ben reached into one of his pockets and took out his Zippo. He flipped it open and thumbed the flint wheel, a bright yellow flame lit up the darkness and above his head another torch jutted out from the wall. He reached up taking it from its holder, placing the lighter beneath it and for a moment it seemed like the flame wouldn't catch, until it gave a little whoosh as it ignited with a puff of black smoke. He placed the Zippo back in his pocket holding the torch out in front of him. A thunderous bang came from the door and it shuddered in its frame. They spun around to see a huge split had formed in the solid oak door, as another horrid roar bellowed through the caverns.

Ben held the torch aloft looking around the room they were now cornered in, and in the flickering light he could just about see another door.

"Come on follow me," he led the way holding Jackie's hand. They reached the door and he placed his shoulder against it and pushed, this time it opened with little effort and they all piled in slamming the door shut behind them, and at that very moment there was a horrendous bang and sound of splintering wood as the demon shattered the door with a mighty kick, it was so tall it had to crouch to get through the doorway. It stood, growling and grunting, its luminous eye piercing through the darkness as it scanned the room.

"Check this out guys, looks like we have a way to fight back," Ben said with a grin. The others stood beside him and couldn't believe their eyes. The room they had just entered was huge and it contained an enormous collection of Medieval memorabilia. All manner of weaponry, suits of armour, shield, flags and other artefacts.

"This must be where they store the exhibits when the tourist season finishes, this stuff must be worth a fortune if not damn priceless," Roger adjusted his glasses, gobsmacked by the incredible collection, when Ben snapped him back to reality.

"I know you love your history Rodge, but this isn't exactly the time for a lesson. Grab whatever weapons you can and get ready, that bastard's gonna come crashing through the door any second,"

They moved quickly, Sarah took a spear, Roger a Mace, Ben and Jackie both grabbed a sword. Ben saw a suit of armour that had its hand clenched as if it were holding a sword or something that was no longer in its grasp.

"Here's what we're gonna do, I'm going to place the torch in its hand, so when that demon comes through the door it'll go straight for this decoy. We'll be hiding in the shadows waiting for it to get clear of the door, when it does, that's when we make a break for it back to that damn portal it came out of, and that's where we make our stand alright," they nodded in agreement as Ben placed the torch in the Knights hand, and they quickly moved towards the door staying hidden as much as possible in the shadows, when Ben was satisfied, they were close enough they came to a stop and waited. From the other room they heard it growl, then it roared and the door shattered beside them, it came in and went straight for the torch light raising its claws high above its head it slashed down sending the suit of armour crashing to the ground in pieces.

The four were running back through the stony corridor, when the howling wind of the vortex pierced through the silence and they emerged back in the room of horror, just in time to witness the bodies of the cult sliding across the floor, being sucked into the glowing whirlpool of doom. A blood curdling roar sent shivers down their spines as the demon came around the corner, they turned to face the horror that now stood glaring down on them, its mighty chest heaving and falling as rage coursed through its body. The four stood there, fear making their hearts pound like the sound of distant drums. They locked eyes with the creature, each waiting for the other to make the first move. The beast screamed raising its fists into the air as its ribcage pulsated, the imprints of something horrid protruded from the skin. With a mighty roar two more arms ripped through the flesh, just beneath the armpits, the four were stunned, mouths agape in awe at what they were witnessing. When the pain subsided, it turned its attention back to them. The vortex was growing stronger with every minute that passed and they could feel themselves being pulled toward it, like invisible hands had seized them by the shoulders their grip growing tighter by the second.

"We're trapped. We can't fight it here that vortex will drag us all in if we're not careful." Ben yelled looking around and noticed another corridor.

"We've got to get away from here, come on," he held out his hand and Jackie took hold. He pushed forward, pulling Jackie along with him, every step was like walking through quick sand with lead weights strapped around their ankles, but onward they struggled until they were thrown forward as the vortex lost its grip. They could hear the creature sinking the clawed fingers of its four arms into the walls dragging itself along. Ben spotted four plinths upon which Suits of armour holding large shields and spears stood guard.

"We don't have much time, get up on those plinths and hide as best you can behind those suits of armour," he helped the others climb onto their ledges before he climbed up on his own and side shuffled, squeezing himself behind the knight, the blade of his sword scraped against the wall with a "skreeek" sound. The demon came hurtling forward as it broke free from the pull of the vortex. It stood silent, looking and listening. A little stone fell from the wall beside Ben and as it hit the ground it bounced, striking the armour with a little "Tinng" the demon turned its head toward the sound and took a step forward. Ben was trembling both from fear and the rush of adrenaline as he gripped the sword with both hands waiting for the beast to discover him. It lifted a hand, stretched out its index finger poking at the armour that swayed back and forth. It turned to leave when it turned back and ripped the suit of armour from its plinth sending it crashing to the floor with a rattling bang. It grabbed Ben around the waist pulling him from his hiding place. He had his sword and raising it above his head drove the tip into the creature's hand. It roared in pain and released him, he dropped to the floor staggering backwards he ended up on his ass. He quickly got to his feet, sword still in hand. When the others jumped from their hiding places to stand beside him.

"I have an idea," he handed his sword to Jackie and quickly bent and picked up the spear that had fallen from the Knight's grasp. The demon came charging toward them when Ben drew back his hand and with a single step launched the spear through the air and the thing roared in agony as the spear jutted from its hideous eye. It staggered left and right bouncing off walls, before one of its arms reached up ripping the spear from its eye that left a gaping hole and a greenish liquid that trickled from the wound.

"Get behind it quickly, Jackie pass me my sword," Ben barked as they ran past the blinded Cyclops taking up positions behind it.

"Sarah, use your spear and stab it in the ribs, I'll worry about its arms. Roger, Jackie you two, attack its legs," he stopped talking when it blindly slashed at the air. One arm came slashing toward Ben, raising the sword he brought it across his body in a dazzling arc and the blade amputated the arm at the elbow. The Cyclops roared as agony ripped through its body as more greenish blue blood spurted from the wound. While it was distracted Sarah jabbed at its ribs with her spear and it took a step backward its last right arm slashing out. She stepped back as the claws flashed by her and stepped forward ramming the spear into it again. Another arm came slashing through the air, and as before Ben took it off with a huge swing of his blade. Roger went rushing in with mace held across his body and with a big swing, the spiked club hit the beast in the knee and it buckled from the pain. Jackie didn't see another hand shooting forward from the shadows, but Ben did. He flipped the sword upward so he was holding it by the blade, drawing his arm back he threw it tumbling end over end through the air and it hit the demon in the eye again, it fell backward onto its back and lay roaring and growling kicking and slashing. Ben lost his temper and ran as fast as he could and jumped. He flew through the air with a bellowing battle cry arms out stretched. He landed on top of the demon and brought both his hands down on the sword driving it through the eye with an eruption of that greenish tinted blood. It tried to grab at him but he pushed the blade further in screaming

"Die you vicious bastard, Die," he was breathing heavy as the creature's blood dripped from his face. The beast thrashed around as new arms began to sprout from its ribcage its dying roars slowly dying down to mere growls as the life drained out of it. Its arms curled up like those of a dead spider, Ben stood up rage coursing through him, he dismounted the beast and stood at its head. The sword twitched as the eye moved, Ben raised his right leg and screamed as he brought it down on the sword and he felt it go through the skull into the ground. Just then the howling wind of the vortex screamed ever closer, as the demon's body began to tremble.

"Get up on that plinth now," Ben yelled helping Jackie and Sarah onto the ledge, Roger joined them.

"Rodge, get the girls between us and hold on to the crevices in the wall," They pushed the girls between them and Roger placed his right hand into the crevice left arm around Ben's shoulder and Ben placed his right arm around Roger's shoulder and his left arm into a crevice. They had the girls anchored safely between them when they finally felt the power of the vortex pulling at them trying to dislodge them.

"Hold on tight this is going to be close," Ben yelled lowering his head grunting under the pressure of holding on for dear life and his feet being dragged out from under him. As they struggled not to be pulled in, the body of the Cyclops went skating up the corridor and into the vortex where it spun round and round all the ways back to whatever hell it came from.

When the demon finally vanished into the black depths, the vortex began to seal itself shut. Ben and the others could feel the invisible force slowly relinquishing its hold on them until finally it stopped completely. They let out a gasp catching their breath and one by one they jumped down from the plinth.

They looked around and all seemed to be back to normality, as they slowly made their way back to the room where it all started.

Ben shook his head in both rage and disgust.

"Damn fools, what the hell were they thinking, or were they thinking at all." He shook his head.

Jackie and Sarah were all bright eyed, excited and relieved at the same time. Jackie threw her arms around Ben and gave him a huge kiss.

"You really know how to think on your feet Ben Connors, anyone else would have panicked and died trying to stop that thing," she said holding him tight.

"Some second date this turned out to be," Roger shook his head and adjusted his glasses.

Ben laughed.

"Some second date is right, we came here for a picnic and instead had to fight for our lives." Sarah hugged Roger.

"I don't know about you three but this demon slaying has given me an appetite, what do you say we go back up grab the picnic basket and do what we came here to do. I'm absolutely starving now," Ben rubbed his belly.

They all just laughed and left the nightmare behind them, as they emerged into the day-light they had to shield their eyes from the glaring sun. Once their eyes had adjusted, they found the picnic basket just where they had left it an hour ago and set up a nearby picnic table, laughing a kidding around as young people do. But, from the shadows a dark figure loomed.

Satan watched them with keen interest and a terrible grin appeared on his pale lifeless face.

"So, it finally begins. The guardians of the last gateway have united, the time for my triumphant return is here at last after all these centuries," he erupted into maniacal laughter as he walked away slowly disappearing in a cloud of grey smoke.

The four have inadvertently set in motion the countdown to Armageddon and in doing so have placed themselves in great danger, for Satan will stop at nothing to destroy them.

# ALIEN CARNAGE

It was a stormy night, a gale force wind bellowed through the alleyways blowing trash around as far as the eye could see. Thunder roared making the ground shake, lightning streaked through the night sky, turning darkness into light. Torrential rain cascaded from the heavens and made driving conditions treacherous. Vehicles slowed to a crawl; the windscreen wipers unable to cope with the rain that was making visibility poor.

Somewhere above the Earth, a spacecraft was approaching at high speed. It was out of control. Sparks and flames flew from the heat shield as it entered the atmosphere. It was plummeting towards the ground at tremendous speed when a bolt of lightning struck it. The circular ship went into a spin, like a coin being flipped into the air. It crashed through a forest ripping up trees and carving a deep, channel into the ground. It skated along like a stone skimming over water before it stopped with a horrendous bang.

The ship lay there, half buried in the channel it had carved for itself in the earth. It looked like a sleeping silver tortoise. It was smouldering from the damaged engine and fried circuitry. A small hole had been carved in its hull from the lightning strike. Nothing appeared to be moving until a door opened and a set of steps snaked from the craft.

A cloud of white smoke filled the ship's interior, and all that was visible was a faint glow of a low blue luminescent light. A silhouette appeared through the vapour. The mist was too heavy to make out what it was, but it was enormous.

Out of the haze it came, standing at least eight feet tall. The sheer bulk of the beast made the steps shudder and squeak, the heavy rain splashing off its snake like skin. Its strong, muscular, legs pounded the steel steps, its eyes were luminous, glowing like a cat's eyes, three rows of razor-sharp teeth glinted in the faint light illuminating from the ship. The beast reached the bottom step, stretching its arms to the sky as lightning flashed showing only three fingers on each of its hands. The foreign beast roared a terrible shriek that was stifled by the howling wind. It lifted its massive head, sniffed at the air, and then growled, running off at super human speed.

At a bus stop in town, a bus came to a slow halt. The doors open with a gentle hiss, and two teenage girls disembarked.

"We've got to be mad coming out in this Sabrina," One of them said, pulling the collar of her coat up to her cheeks to stop the wind and rain.

"I know we're mad Becky, but who cares? We're here now," The other girl said, placing her hands in her jacket pockets shrugging up her shoulders as the rain drenched them.

Both girls walked off into the night, the storm raging. They walked through the park hoping the trees might give them some protection.

The alien was there too, watching them, so close they could have reached out and touched it.

"Damn its Sabrina this place gives me the creeps. Can we get out of here, please?" One girl said nervously.

"God, will you relax Becky. It's a lousy night, too severe for any weirdo's being out," the other said trying to light up a smoke.

The creature growled, watching them, waiting for the right moment to strike. Saliva dripped from its hideous mouth as it became hungry. Without warning, it roared, coming into view. The girls screamed and ran. The alien watched for a second, then attacked. With super speed, it was on them. One girl looked behind and screamed, as the beast reached out a hand and grabbed her, lifting her off the ground looking at her frightened face growling at her. It hurled her through the air "Becky" the girl screamed as she flew twenty feet landing with a sickening thump.

The other girl kept running unaware that the creature had overtaken her and was now in front of her. She glanced behind her when something made her stop. She turned her head slowly looking forward;

her mouth open and a terrible agony ran through her body paralysing her. She shivered, trying to scream, but the pain was so intense it came out a mere whisper. She looked down, saw the creature's razor-sharp claws had penetrated her stomach, and straight through her back. Blood trickled from her mouth. The alien roared again, pulling its clawed hand back, tearing the intestines out with it. The girl's body collapsed into a bundle at its feet. It sniffed at her, poking at her inquisitively. Its hand dripping with blood, its forked tongue licked at it, the tasted of blood driving it into a frenzy. It roared bending over, and with one bite, it ripped the flesh from her face right to the bone. It dragged the body across the park, laid it beside the other girl, and continued eating, there was sickening ripping sound as it tore of her arms off sinking its teeth into the warm flesh stripping it from the bone.

By the time it finished, there was only a horrible, bloody mess left. It walked off into the shadows. The other girl was only knocked out and woke up dazed and confused. As she came around, her eyes rolled lazily as she focused on her surroundings. When her vision cleared, what was before her sent her body into tremors, she opened her mouth to scream, but no sound came out she looked at the butchered mess beside her. The alien appeared, towering over her, it swung its clawed hand, and blood gushed from her severed throat. It ate again, and by the time, it finished, fragments of severed flesh, partial limbs, blood, and flesh ragged bones were all that remained. It then disappeared into the night, its hunger satisfied, at least for the meantime.

*The next morning:*

Roger and Sarah arrived at Jackie's place for breakfast. They were drinking coffee when the television reporter described the gruesome scene at the park.

"Hey, look at this!" Sarah turned up the volume.

The reporter was clearly shaken by what she had seen. "This is Cindy Shields reporting live from MacArthur Park, where, earlier today a jogger named John Sherman made a shocking and gruesome discovery. At 6.30, this morning while out for his regular morning run, he came across the butchered remains of what seemed to be two bodies. They are so mutilated that police forensics don't know which body parts belong to whom. The victims appear to have been in the park seeking refuge from last night's severe storm, when they were brutally murdered. Police have declined to comment on this matter, only saying they are following a definite line of inquiry. Will this lunatic strike again? Only time will tell. This is Cindy Shields for A-B-C-7 news," she glanced behind her as two body bags were wheeled off to the waiting coroner's vehicle.

Ben turned off the TV and sat.

"God almighty, who or what could do something like that?"

Jackie looked at Sarah.

"I don't know how they can even sleep after doing that to someone."

Sarah said in disgust. Ben and Roger said nothing.

*Back in the city:*

Two city workers were doing a routine check on the sewer system. They split up to check different sections. One of them was whistling when something moved behind him. He spun around, but there was nothing there. He looked startled when something moved again.

"Damn, this is creepy," he said to himself.

Without warning, a large rat ran, screaming past him. He gave a frightened yelp, gasped for breath then laughed. The laughter didn't last for long. His flashlight shone on the ground and he saw strange footprints in the sediment and slime, the likes of which he'd never seen.

"What the hell. Those aren't rat prints," he bent over to get a closer look, and slowly began to followed the footprints.

Twenty meters in he came to a sudden halt when he heard something move behind him. He looked around in a panic, his heart pounding as he shone his torch in front of him. Something was standing there growling, its teeth shining in the light. The man yelped and ran away, panicking and panting, with sweat soaking his face, the torch flew from his grasp tumbling end over end as the creature crashed into him knocking him to the ground with a heavy thump that knocked the wind clean out of him.

At the opposite end of the sewer, the other man was finishing his safety checks when he thought he heard a faint scream. He took the two-way radio from his utility belt pushed the button and spoke.

"Are you okay Dave, thought I heard you yell something?" Taking his finger off the button, he listened. There was nothing but static.

He walked through the tunnel towards the other man's position and had gone sixty feet in when something glistened in the beam of his flashlight. He bent down and with his gloved hand ran his fingers through it bringing it closer to his face and then realized it was blood.

"Dave, are you alright? Where are you?" He screamed, his voice echoing through the sewer.

He continued walking along when he stopped dead in his tracks. There was a man's body or what remained of it impaled on a steel pipe. He tried to run, but slipped on something. It was the other man's insides. He screamed as he tried to get back on his feet. When he tried to run, the creature came rushing out of the shadows swinging its claws. The man tried to scream, but only a gurgling sound came as blood poured from his mouth.

His hands clutched around his severed throat, he looked up in horror. The beast roared swinging its claws again the last thing he saw, were the hideous teeth and eyes then everything went black.

There was panic all over town as reports of a U.F.O. crash in a nearby forest flooded the airways and television stations. Ben, Jackie, Roger, and Sarah were in town when they heard the news.

"You've got to be joking," Ben exclaimed as they watched the drama unfold on a television in an electronics store window.

Helicopter shots of the U.F.O. filled the screen, he could not believe it.

"Why are we standing here? Let's go check it out for ourselves," he said as they ran back to his car piled in and sped off to the site.

When they arrived, the police had roadblocks in place and traffic was being diverted.

"We have to get in there," Jackie said, looking around.

"Is there another way to get in without being noticed?" Roger looked up to the sky, which was full of TV helicopters.

"Drive on for another mile and take the next left," Sarah said, breaking the silence.

The engine of the dark blue Mustang roared; the tires screeched as Ben stamped on the accelerator. They turned off the Free way and down a long dirt road. There didn't appear to be any sign of police activity in the area. The car came to a screeching halt when Ben hit the brakes and they got out.

"Where do we go from here? We need to get close enough to take a look at the spaceship," Ben said clicking on his flashlight.

They climbed over a wooden gate and walked into the dense forest staying close together, their lights moving left-to-right scanning everything. They hadn't gone too far when they heard a police two-way radio. They turned off their torches quickly taking cover behind a clump of trees. Two police officers came into view. They were carrying pump-action shotguns loaded and ready.

"I can't believe a God dam alien could be responsible for those murders in the park. We found the ship, and I still don't believe it," a tall, lean, faced cop said as his partner shone his torch into the trees.

"Yeah, I hear you buddy. I never believed in extra-terrestrials before tonight, but I do now. We better tell the Chief to leave guards at all the phone booths in the city," he said smiling.

"Why would we want to do that?" The other cop asked with a puzzled look on his face.

"In case, this bastard tries to phone home." Their laughter and footsteps faded into the distance.

Jackie switched on her light and emerged from behind the clump of trees.

"They're gone," she beckoned to the others.

Three more light beams appeared beside her.

"We're getting close. Let's keep going," Roger said, and they moved on toward the crash site.

Ten minutes later, they appeared on top of a ridge, and looked in awe at the scene unfolding below. There, in full view was a circular ship half buried in the earth, with a trail of destruction behind it where it crashed the previous night. The dome like structure of the roof resembled a shining silver turtle shell protruding from the deep channel.

"God almighty, there it is," Sarah exclaimed with amazement in her voice.

Below them, there were lots of activities. People in yellow Hazmat suits walked around the ship, others in white suits examining the interior. Around the craft, armed police officers stood guard. The National Guard was there also. Soldiers were given orders to "Shoot to kill on sight," by their commanding officer.

Just then, something moved in the woods behind them, and Ben turned to see what it was. There was nothing, only blackness. He was just turning away when something ran at lightning speed toward the ship; he couldn't figure out what it was, he only saw a shadow.

"Christ, it's here," he said, pointing his finger to the ship.

Within seconds, screams of terror came from below, He and the others ran as fast as they could back into the woods, and made their way to the site staying hidden in the trees and bushes. Gunfire echoed, their muzzle flashes looking like fireworks on the fourth of July. The screaming and firing continued for over ten minutes then there was silence. The four walked from the woods into the site.

"God, they're dead, they've been torn apart," Roger said with shock and fear in his voice.

Everywhere they looked, Mutilated bodies, severed limbs and buckets of blood littered the area. The floodlights around the ship made the situation even more terrifying, casting shadows around their feet.

"Everyone, be cautious because that thing could still be here," Ben said, bending over, picking up a dead soldier's machine gun.

Suddenly, something ran past them so fast they only saw a shadow.

"It's here," Ben, screamed firing a few shots into the darkness. He stood there with the gun pushed hard to his shoulder, his heart pounding out of his chest. It came running from the shadows roaring.

"Holy shit," Jackie yelled as she came to Ben's side.

He pushed her out of the way as the alien rushed at them. He fell to the ground, rolling out of its path as it raced past.

"It's heading back to the town, we have to get back to the car," Ben barked as he dropped the gun and they ran back through the forest, their hearts pounding into the night knowing that the beast could be anywhere.

If it was heading toward the city, it was going to be a blood bath, and the Military had failed to stop it, so it was up to our heroes to take this thing down now.

They were running as fast as they could, heading back to the car when Sarah yelled, falling flat on her face.

"Up you get", Ben, said helping her to her feet.

They jumped over the gate and climbed into the Mustang.

The car roared down the dirt road, the rear end fishtailed as Ben turned the wheel to get on to the Free way. In the distance lightning flashed and thunder rumbled.

"Did you see the size of that thing?" Roger gasped for breath.

"Oh, we saw it all right," Jackie cupped her hands over her mouth.

Sarah hugged Roger. She was scared. They were all scared.

"Whatever that thing is, it's got to be destroyed before it destroys us," Ben said shifting gear.

Lightning flashed again, and rain poured down hard.

The lights of the city came into view, and within fifteen minutes, they were there. Ben slowed the Mustang, and they looked for any sign of the Alien. It ran out in front of them, and they screamed. Ben gave a sharp turn of the wheel trying to hit the creature. He jammed on the brakes as it disappeared down a side alley.

"Is everyone all right?" He unfastened his seat belt and got out of the car.

The others stood beside him. Suddenly, a scream came from the alley. They raced over and saw the body of a man with his throat torn out. The beast bolted from the shadows, crashing through a wire fence into Ronald's auto wrecking yard.

"After it," Jackie yelled and they gave chase.

Scrapped and crushed cars lined the yard as far as the eye could see. It was like a maze. Lightning struck a power line, making it explode in a shower of sparks. The rain pelted down with unrelenting force. Ben looked up and saw a giant crane used to lower the cars into the crusher.

"I have an idea," he said, wiping the water from his eyes.

"Lightning always strikes the tallest object first, right?" he added.

"Yeah," Sarah said looking confused.

"Here's what we're going to do. If we can lure it beneath the crane, and hook it with the grabber, hoist it up as high as the boom will take it, then we can let the lightning do the rest. I'll be the bait and get that thing to follow me," he said.

"It'll kill you," Jackie screamed, grabbing his arm.

"It'll kill us all and many more if we don't do this now. Get moving, we don't have much time," Ben ordered, kissing her, and took off into the maze of scrap.

Jackie, Roger, and Sarah climbed the crane.

Ben sauntered into the maze, looking around him. The alien was watching him from high above on a mountain of scrap metal, saliva dripping from its terrifying teeth, Ben's reflection in its eyes. It slashed its claws through the air; they ripped into the metal as Ben screamed.

"Hey. Here I am."

His voice echoed through the mountains of scrap. The others had reached the top of the crane and had a bird's-eye view of everything from where they were. Ben was like a dot in the distance. The beast attacked climbing down the pile of crushed cars right towards Ben.

"Oh fuck," he yelled and ran.

The creature was right behind him. Ben was weaving left and right, dodging its attack. It swung its claws, and he heard a ripping noise as the claws cut through his denim jacket.

Jackie opened the door of the cab and stepped out onto the platform, cupping her hands over her mouth she yelled "Turn right,".

Ben ran as fast as he could, but he tripped and fell over, tumbling to the ground. He looked up with terror in his eyes as the alien stood looking at him.

"Ben," Jackie yelled, seeing him fall.

"What are you waiting for you, son of a bitch?" He barked staring the alien in the face.

The creature lunged at him, its hand clamped around his throat, lifting him off the ground. He tried to struggle free, but it was too strong, he lashed out kicking it repeatedly in the face until it released him. He gasped for breath as the thing roared, running, and crashing into him, sending him flying across the ground. Ben rolled under a pyramid of crushed cars and waited. The alien dropped to its knees its clawed hands reached under trying to grab him.

"Damn, this thing never gives up," he said, moving away from its claws.

He swallowed hard as their eyes locked on each other. He rolled out from beneath the cars on the opposite side, getting to his feet. A heavy crash made him look up, and there fifteen feet above him was the monster. It lifted a car from the pile, and screamed, sending the car crashing into the ground, where Ben had been only moments ago. He jumped out the way before it hit and was now running toward the crane.

Lightning streaked from the sky; the rain was battering Ben. As he was running, he could hear the beast leaping across the mountains of metal.

"That's it, you ugly mother fucker, keep coming," he said with a grin, running faster with thunder crashing overhead sending vibrations through the ground.

The beast roared, closing in on Ben when through the pounding rain and thunder he heard an engine rumble to life. He stopped dead and turned to face the creature.

"You want me well here I am," as the beast strode toward him the metal claws dropped from above and closed around the Aliens waist. It went crazy trying to prise the claws from its body as it was slowly lifted into the air. No amount of struggling was going to save it now. Ben placed his hand over his eyes to shield them from the driving rain but all he could see was a mere silhouette struggling high above the city. Its screams became louder and as it clawed and thrashed about, a blinding flash struck the arm of the crane and thousands of volts of electricity coursed through its body

It roared, swinging its arms in agony as another bolt of lightning struck it. Again, it roared. One of its arms fell to the ground amputated by the extreme voltage. The skin smouldered and blistered. Agonizing roars could be heard for miles. The group in the crane looked on as another lightning bolt struck the creature making it burst into flames. Blue blood spurted from its mouth and with one last bolt, Roger who was at the controls opened the claws and the creature plummeted 120 feet landing with a sickening bang. Roger, Jackie, and Sarah climbed down the ladder. When they got to the ground, they could see it still smouldering. Its bright blue blood sprayed everywhere.

"It's over," Ben put his arm around Jackie.

Suddenly, a huge orange tinted light hovered overhead and a red beam streamed from it.

"You've got to be kidding," Roger, said eyes fixed on the circular ship hovering above.

The red light surrounded the dead alien's body, lifting it into the ship. The craft hovered there for a few seconds before it lifted off and zoomed off into the great unknown.

"Let's go home," Jackie said as they walked back to the car and drove off into the night.

*Several months later:*

On a top-secret Military base somewhere in the Nevada desert, the ship lay locked in a massive hangar. Inside the craft in a hidden compartment strings of a vile gooey viscous substance that criss crossed like a spider's web began to pulsate and stretch. The membrane that encased the thing began to rip as a three fingered clawed hand tore through followed by the other. The hands grabbed the membrane ripping it open and the alien creature stepped out dripping with a clear mucus substance that pooled at its feet, high up in the ceiling a little red linked blinked, it was a surveillance camera and monitoring the proceedings from the safety of a control room a man in formal Military dress sat in the shadows a red glow emanated from where he was seated as he took a long drag from his Cuban cigar watching the creature on screen.

"You may proceed with the capture and containment Private," he ordered a young man who wore a microphone headset.

"Yes, sir General sir," he pushed a button on the side of his headset

"Platoon move in, capture and containment is a go repeat capture and containment is a go,"

As it took in its surroundings, a door hissed open and soldiers dressed in yellow Hazmat suits rushed in with tranquillizer guns, shock sticks, and flash grenades. The creature tried to fight them off but to no avail, it was still too weak after just being born so it was relatively easy to subdue, one man took a flash grenade and removed the pin, he rolled it across the floor where it exploded with a loud bang and massive orange flash, the creature squealed shaking its head placing its hands up to its dazed eyes as it staggered backward. Six soldiers dropped to one knee and took aim, and with a "fhht, fhht, fhht" sound the tranquillizer darts flew through the air. They hit their target and within seconds the alien staggered and wobbled on its weakening legs. Six more darts flew hit their mark, twelve darts stuck fast to the creature pumping their anaesthetic into its system. It took one rickety step forward and collapsed in heap on the cold steel floor. Other soldiers moved in binding its hands and feet with steel manacles. Over the radio in the control room the Private turned to his commanding officer.

"Capture and containment successful General," he saluted the man who stood, crushing out his cigar, placing his hat on his head adjusting it.

"Excellent work men, take our guest to the laboratory. Today is a great day for the Military and for America. Operation Desert Moon is a go. Do we have our test subjects ready for our little experiment?" he asked placing his hands behind his back.

"Yes, sir they are prepped and ready for the doctors," The Private said with a little apprehension in his voice.

"Cheer up son, you should be proud to be part of this new miracle era for the army. If this goes according to plan, then we will have the most powerful, unstoppable soldiers in the world." He saluted the

Private and left the room.

As he marched down a long dimly lit corridor, he bumped into a man called Major Tom Sykes and stopped to talk with him.

"My god Tom, this is it. This is what we've been waiting for all these years, and today will go down in history as one of the finest moments since we put men on the moon. Why don't you come with me Tom and bear witness to this new era of Military might, if we can successfully implant alien DNA into a human, they will have speed, agility and strength, the likes of which the world has never seen. Come with me Tom, you will be perfectly safe. There's nine inches of bullet proof glass to separate us from the test subjects should anything go wrong," he waited for the reply.

"You finally get your operation Desert Moon General, good for you, but I for one do not approve nor support your experiment Sir." He turned and stormed off down the hall.

The General was furious.

"I don't care if you approve or not Major, I've waited for this opportunity all my life and now that we're so close to finally realizing my dream nothing is going to stop me. Desert Moon will be a success just you wait and see," he said to himself as he marched down the hall toward the test area.

# RISE OF THE FOUR

## NIGHT OF THE CHAINSAW

Harry Gordon was a Lumberjack. He stood six feet nine inches with a strong, muscular build. He could cut down any tree in less than ten minutes with an axe. Such was his strength that his fellow workers called him "the Hulk". The company he worked for, Kentwood Logging, was on a two-year contract in an isolated part of Alaska, where the only way in or out was by helicopter. The crew of thirty men started work in the forest at seven every morning. Chainsaws would roar, echoing for miles around. Trees would squeak and creak as they tumbled to the ground before being dragged off to be de-branched, and the bare log hoisted onto the ever-increasing pile of lumber. They spent ten months working in freezing conditions. The loneliness and isolation getting to every man there. The separation was hardest on Harry, for one fateful morning, he received a letter from his fiancée saying they were finished, and enclosed with the letter was the diamond ring he'd given her twelve months earlier. Harry crumpled up the letter and threw it to the ground storming off in a rage.

For weeks after he barely spoke to anyone. His mental condition was suffering.

One day, while cutting down a tree, two of his fellow workers heard him talking to himself and what he was saying scared them.

"Bastards, I'll kill them all kill them, I will. They made me lose everything. Now they will pay."

Harry screamed, his axe dealing the final blow, and the tree came crashing down with a thump.

He stood there, axe gripped in both hands, his breath steaming in the cold air, he cast an evil stare at the two men, and they grew nervous. One of them asked, "Are you okay, Harry?"

Tim Mullins was a fifty-five-year-old lumberjack who had been in the logging industry the last twenty-five years. His slender frame trembled as Harry laughed an evil laugh, turning to face the man who spoke. His eyes were wild and angry, his teeth clenched in anger. The two men walked away from him.

When they got back to their campsite, they reported what had happened to their supervisor.

Harry returned to the camp three hours later and at once was summoned to the supervisor's office.

Jonathon Kentwood sat at his desk smoking a cigar. He was typing on his computer when the door opened and in walked Harry.

"Sit down Harry," he said, placing the cigar on the edge of the table.

"I'd rather stand," Harry growled in a low husky voice.

"Suit yourself," Jonathon said, looking at him puzzled.

"Harry you're a good worker, you're the best worker we have, but the men are nervous around you lately, and I don't want my workers feeling threatened by anyone. What happened out there today, Harry? Tim came to me, and he was very shaken up saying you acted all crazy. What's with you?" Jonathon asked as he walked from behind the desk to sit right in front of Harry who was breathing hard. Harry felt like he could tear this man apart there and then, as his fists clenched, he swallowed hard trying to keep control of himself.

"I'm sorry Harry, but you haven't been yourself as of late, so I'm afraid I have to let you go. There's a helicopter bringing supplies in the morning. I want you on that chopper and out of here. Get back to civilization and get professional Psychiatric help," Kentwood said handing him a check. Harry's eyes opened wide, his hulking figure moving toward the man.

"Kentwood, I will make you suffer for this, that I promise you," he growled, looking down on the man with terrifying eyes, then turning, he walked out from the room.

That night while Harry slept a voice from his dreams spoke to him.

"Harry, H-A-R-R-Y," it called.

"Yes," Harry moaned turning on his side.

"Harry, do you want to make them suffer for this humiliation?" the voice said.

"I'd kill them if I could. I'd give my soul to the Devil just to have my revenge," he replied clenching his fist.

The voice laughed and Harry woke up startled. "Come outside Harry," the voice called as the cabin door creaked open.

A blizzard had started and blinding snow melted on his warm face.

"Where are you?" Harry screamed over the howling wind.

"Harry, I'm over here," the voice spoke again, this time a bright light shone in the distance, and he followed it.

His huge, muscular legs pushed through the snow; snowflakes clung to his long beard. As he got closer, he noticed the light was coming from a cave. He entered and could see nothing until the ghostly voice spoke again.

"Harry, think of what your lover has done to you, of how your supervisor humiliated you, how the others told tales about you. Are you going to let them get away with that?"

Harry's rage exploded.

"No, I will not let them get away with it," he roared while the voice laughed.

"Will you give me your soul if I give you your revenge? If I make you a killing machine?" the voice said taunting him.

"My soul died a long time ago and you're welcome to it," Harry barked his breathing becoming faster.

"Harry. Vengeance will be yours tonight and for evermore," the voice said then a blinding light appeared.

He put his hands up to his eyes, the light was so intense. It died down after a second or two, and there upon a rock rested a chainsaw. It was pure silver, and it radiated with evil.

"Pick it up Harry. Just take it and revenge will be yours," the voice said.

Harry reached out his hands to pick up the saw, but he hesitated. He felt fear. A cold sweat appeared on his brow reaching out his trembling hands again to seize the machine of death, but he pulled them back sensing the evil that now surrounded him.

"Do not fear it my boy, just pick it up," the voice taunted him to take the gleaming, sinister machine.

Harry's rage went off the scale; he seized the chainsaw with both hands. The voice laughed again, and Harry screamed and shook. The chainsaw started up with a mighty roar. He screamed as the saw, which seemed to have a life of its own, turned on him, it broke free from his grasp and hovered in mid-air, then at lightning speed it attacked. The machine was just a blur as it carved into his flesh over and over. Agony appeared across his face, as the whirring serrated chain cut his face and body to ribbons, as if it was being guided by a phantom force. He screamed in agony as blood dripped from the evil blade. For what seemed like an eternity, it kept cutting into him until it stopped, and floated back down coming to rest on the rock. He was on all fours, torn rags of flesh dangling from his back, the silver blade dripping with blood that seemed to trickle backward into the blade as if the machine was drinking it. He was breathing deeply and shaking badly when an intense light came from the blade cocooning him in its glow. He screamed as his injuries began to heal instantaneously. After a while, the light disappeared, and he got to his feet. His face and body were distorted and twisted, scarred all over; he no longer looked human, but resembled a wrinkled, and scratched, worn piece of leather, like a zombie from a George Romero movie. He growled, then, roared picking up the weapon again.

"Well done, Harry," a man said, clapping his hands emerging from the shadows.

"What have you done to me?" He barked.

"You gave me your soul and I have given revenge to you. This machine has amazing powers. It can heal you when you are injured, you can never die," the stranger grinned.

"I can live forever?" Harry asked.

"Forever Harry. The power of the blade can keep you alive forever as long as you keep it by your side. If you lose the chainsaw, then you lose your immortality. You are my soul harvester now Harry. Go out there and send them to hell," the stranger yelled disappearing into a cloud of smoke.

Harry's eyes burned bright red, glowing embers coming out of the dark. The chainsaw roared as he held it high above his head screaming. He was now a creature of evil, neither alive, but neither dead nor dying. He was now a chainsaw wielding modern-day Grim Reaper. The silver blade glistened in the faint moonlight as he pushed his way through the snow back to the campsite.

Tim Mullins lay sleeping, when the door of his cabin shattered from a mighty kick. He woke with a jump.

"What the hell is going on here?" He yelped his tired eyes looking at the shattered door.

Harry just laughed, walking toward the frightened man. A look of horror appeared on the man's face as the blood machine roared into action.

"Dear God, no," he screamed, the silver blade sparkling in the pale moonlight.

Screams of agony echoed into the night waking the rest of the loggers. They ran to the cabin where a gruesome sight awaited them.

"Tim?" a man asked entering the cabin.

He was sickened when he saw Tim Mullins lying in his blood-soaked bed. He had been cut in half. His intestines dangled to the floor while his legs were on the other side of the room. The other workers gathered outside Mullins's cabin. Jim Sutton, the second person who saw Harry's rage with Tim Mullins the day before, appeared in the doorway, looking as white as snow. Suddenly, Harry charged from the shadows the chainsaw roaring. Sutton turned around, startled, and the last thing he witnessed before his demise was a flash of light from the blade, his head rolled down the three steps landing at the other worker's feet. Fear and panic ran through them as Harry revved up the engine cutting a running man's legs from under him. The man screamed as the serrated chain ripped through his stomach. Blood flew from his mouth and Harry laughed.

The men ran for their lives from this maniac, but they didn't get far. One by one, they fell under Harry's rage. Screams of terror echoed into the night, followed by the chilling roar of the chainsaw.

For the next two hours, the screams continued. Then there was silence.

Blood had turned the snow red; body parts littered the site. Harry ambled through the gruesome mess. His evil eyes scanned everywhere, his breath steaming in the cold air. Jonathon Kentwood trembled in the shadows as he watched in terror the horrifying scene in front of him. His heart pounding so loud he thought this mad man might hear it. Harry walked past where he was hiding; Jonathon slapped his hands over his mouth to stifle a scream. He watched Harry walk by into the distance before running from his hiding place in a panic. His large, heavy body made running through the snow difficult. He sank waist deep into a snowdrift. Whining and whimpering as he struggled to get himself free, but his hands only pushed more snow in around him. Suddenly he stopped with fear across his face. He could hear heavy footfalls crunching the snow underfoot. He heard a low, husky, gravelly voice as Harry stood behind him.

"I told you I'd make you suffer you son of a bitch. Now join the others in death," He yelled and the whirring blade roared to life.

Kentwood screamed in agony, blood spraying from his head splashing across Harry's face. He laughed insanely, watching the chainsaw cut through the half-buried man, splitting him open like a banana peel. Harry stood there, rage flowing through him like electricity, making him tremble. He reared his head back and screamed.

The next morning a faint whirring sound echoed in the distance:

The helicopter was approaching. Harry was hiding in the woods nearby as the helicopter came into land. The rotor blades blew the snow around as it landed on the helipad. The man switched off the engine, the rotor blades came to a gentle stop. Unbuckling his seat belt, he opened the door and climbed out. Harry knew the pilot was his only chance of leaving this remote site.

"Hello. Is anybody there?" Sam King yelled, cupping his hands over his mouth as he called out.

He thought it was strange that it was quiet; usually when he arrived, the place would be buzzing like a hornet's nest with chainsaws roaring everywhere, but not today. He took off his sunglasses and looked around before strolling into the camp.

Log cabins filled the area left and right and when he went around the corner of one cabin, he spied a mutilated body on the ground.

"Christ almighty," He whispered while he made the sign of the cross, turned away vomiting violently.

He staggered his way back to the chopper. He was reaching out his hand to open the door when Harry appeared behind him roaring as the man turned Harry made a huge fist and pounded the man's face cutting him open under his left eye. Sam bounced off the helicopter from the force of the impact. His dazed blurred vision stared hazily up at Harry towering over him, he reached down, grabbing the man by the jacket ripping him to his feet, pinning him to the chopper.

"You will take me from here to the mainland," He screamed at the pilot.

Sam looked up at the disfigured mutilated maniac. "And if I don't?" he said, gasping for breath.

The saw roared and Harry held the whirring blade in front of Sam's face edging it closer and closer.

"All right, all right, I'll take you back," Sam, cried as the engine stopped and both men climbed into the helicopter.

Sam felt sick and dizzy from the unreal power of this lunatic, also from fear. Harry was sitting beside him.

"Fly or die," he barked putting the death chain across Sam's throat.

The engine hummed the rotor blades turned. In a few short minutes, the helicopter lifted off and flew into the morning sun.

They were half way through their journey, when Sam passed out, his eyes rolled back into his head his breathing was fast. His hands slipped from the joystick; the helicopter went out of control.

"Stay awake," Harry, demanded, grabbing him by the coat collar, shaking the hell out of him. Sam came too, shook his head to clear his vision, and brought the helicopter back under control. Only another thirty minutes and they would be back on the mainland. From high above, Harry could see the docks with fishing trawlers and cargo ships anchored.

"Set us down now," he yelled and the helicopter began its slow descent.

When it landed, Harry fired up the motor and smiled

"Thank you for flying Gordon Airways. I hope you enjoyed your flight, now fucking die," He yelled as Sam screamed, his blood spraying across the windows and his headless body fell over on Gordon's shoulder.

Harry pushed it off and got out. He ran off into the woods beside the docks. He spotted a ship "The Los Angeles Star".

"Los Angeles! That cheating bitch is there," He growled to himself recalling his fiancée. The ship's gangway was lowered and Harry ran up it, the instrument of death held firmly in his left hand, he hid behind some crates as crew members went about their work oblivious of his presence. He spied an open door and with one last glance around, he made a dash for it. He ran to the cargo hold and hid in the darkest corner he could find.

After an hour, the crew finished loading, and the cargo doors closed with a bang. The ship's engine roared, the vessel lurching as it moved. He was coming back, back for revenge, and another bloodthirsty rampage was about to begin.

Ben and Jackie were up late, lying together on the black leather couch in a loving embrace. It was two in the morning and they were watching night of the living dead. Ben looked into her deep ocean blue eyes.

"You know something, Jackie," he said running his fingers through her hair.

"And what's that I should know?" She whispered, smiling up at him.

"I love you more than you could ever know and that I'll always protect you no matter what monsters and demons we encounter" he kissed her forehead and smiled.

She looked at him raising her head and kissed him.

"I know you wouldn't let anything happen to me Ben and I love you too." She turned over and lay on top of him he reached his hands around grabbing her buttocks.

"Now my dear what do you say we call it a night and get to bed because right now I need a good banging," she kissed his neck climbed off and ran up the stairs. He grabbed the remote control and switched off the TV threw it back on the couch and ran up the stairs to the bed room to find Jackie naked. He stripped off, jumped onto the bed and kissed her passionately.

As they made love, somewhere at sea, all hell had broken loose on board the Los Angeles Star.

Sailors ran in all directions, as lightning flashed and the sea roared, sending thirty-foot waves crashing into the vessel. In the midst of the chaos, a chainsaw could be heard, followed by terrible blood curdling screams. Harry had been discovered in the cargo hold and he went crazy.

He'd butchered sixteen crew men, and the remaining twenty-six ran for their lives. Up on the bridge, the captain was on the radio trying to call the coast guard. All he got back was static. The storm played havoc with the electrics. He switched a button on the radio that would send a repeat may day to the coast guard.

Driving rain battered the crew, and Harry's hulking figure appeared in the dim lights on the deck of the ship. Decapitated bodies fell under the saw's blade. Men jumped from the ship to avoid a grisly death. But Harry kept coming. Their screams only drove him on even more. He liked killing now. Only three remained alive, he was hunting them.

"Come out, come out where ever you are," he said with an evil laugh.

A terrified man ran from the shadows. The saw roared again and his head dropped to the ground, making the upright body dance and twitch as it spurted blood everywhere. The captain and his first mate were running down the steel steps to the cargo hold. Their heavy footsteps reached Harry's ears.

"Ah! There you are," he said with a lopsided grin, walking to where the sound had emanated.

Harry liked to intimidate his victims, so he walked down the stairs, pounding his feet on every step to frighten the men even more.

Inside the cargo hold, only darkness awaited. The captain and the other man hid in the shadows. The steel door creaked open, and Harry walked in, shutting it tight behind him.

"You're not afraid of the dark, are you?" he asked with a laugh.

The chainsaw roared into action. He put the blade across a metal railing sending sparks flying. The sparks lit up the whole area, illuminating the shadow of a man. Harry ran screaming at the figure with the chainsaw roaring. The man yelled, putting his arms in front of his face in a reaction of horror, and with one whip of the whirring blade, the arms fell to the ground as he screamed in agony, blood gushing from the wounds. The saw revved again, the sailor's screams pierced through the captain's ears, and he placed his hands over them to stop the terror. The engine stopped roaring, and became a low sputtering hum, still running with blood dripping from the blade. There was nothing left of the man only bits of mangled, butchered flesh and bone.

"Ah! The sound of torture is music to my ears," Harry laughed, and continued:

"Now it's your turn to scream," he barked as the captain panicked, running for the door yelling a frightened yelp.

He was trying hard to unlock the bulkhead door, but Harry had sealed it tight. The man trembled with fear turning around slowly with terror-stricken eyes Harry's hand clamped around his throat, lifting him off the ground, slamming his head into the bulk-head three times. The man coughed and gagged for breath, trying to break free from the madman's grasp, he let him go and the captain leaned against the bulk-head to stop himself from falling over. Harry only laughed, and brought the chainsaw up between the man's legs slicing through him. The man's body shook, and bled, as the machine, finally cut through the top of his skull. The body split in two collapsing on either side of him.

"That's what you call a split personality," he said his insane laughter echoing through the cargo hold, as he opened the door.

For the next two days, he sat in the bridge until the ship trembled. It had gone aground. With a mighty jolt, Harry was thrown out of the seat landing with a heavy thump. He got to his feet, and picked up his instrument of death. He ran to the deck of the ship, and launched a lifeboat. With the saw by his side, he picked up the oars and rowed as he sang:

"Row, row, row your boat gently down the stream. Harry Gordon's back in town and now you're going to scream," he laughed and laughed, as he landed on the deserted beach taking shelter in a cave until dark...

Ben, Jackie, Roger, and Sarah walked down the dark road that led from Sarah and Jackie's homes. The towering trees and dim street lights made the place seem eerie. Ben and Jackie walked with arms around each other, Roger and Sarah walked beside them. They were talking about the long week's work they've all had.

Roger was now running his own computer repair shop and was doing great. Jackie was a journalist with her own agony aunt column in the local paper "L.A. Now." Sarah ran her own fitness gym called "Energize." and Ben was a factory worker, for a car manufacturer. As they walked along, Ben halted, fumbling around in his jacket pocket.

"What are you doing?" Sarah asked with a smile.

"Just give me a second here. I have it," Ben replied with a huge grin.

"Jackie close your eyes and don't open them until I tell you," he said, taking a beautiful diamond ring from his pocket.

She had her eyes closed tight, smiling all the time. Ben got down on one knee, holding her hand.

"You can open your eyes now." Her eyes opened, and she was left breathless.

He looked up at her.

"Jackie, will you marry me?" He asked his heart racing faster with each second that passed.

She took a deep breath to contain her excitement. Ben stood not knowing what to do next, and that's when he saw her deep blue eyes sparkling brighter than the diamond on her ring.

"Yes," she screamed, jumping up, throwing her arms around him, and kissing him.

He slid the ring onto her finger and placed the box back in his pocket. She threw her arms around him and kissed him again. Sarah and Roger hugged them both, giving them their congratulations.

"This is fantastic. Let's go party. And I know just the place," Sarah exclaimed with delight.

"And where's that?" Roger said, catching her hand.

"Well, it's been a year since we met, so why not go back to where it began? The Aces High," Sarah's eyes were gleaming.

"That's a nice idea, Sarah. I didn't know you could be that romantic," Roger said hugging her.

They walked off into the night, unaware of the nightmare that awaited them.

Harry prowled in the shadows outside his ex-fiancée's bathroom window. Her silhouette shone through the glass. His huge hands gripped the chainsaw tightly as another silhouette appeared that of a man. His eyes burned with a terrible rage, and he waited and watched. After a while, the two silhouettes appeared again and one of them switched off the bathroom light. Harry ran from the shadows to the kitchen window and peered inside. He saw them kissing, and the chainsaw screamed. The man and the woman jumped as Harry kicked in the door. He revved the engine and attacked. The man tried to wrestle him to the ground, but Harry's strength was extraordinary. The blade flashed, and the man's ivory bathrobe turned red. Harry went berserk cutting him to pieces and the engine stopped. He marched from the kitchen up the stairs to her bedroom.

"Amanda, where are you hiding you back-stabbing bitch?" he screamed shattering the bedroom door with a mighty kick.

She was hiding under the bed, biting her clenched fist to stop herself screaming. Harry's feet were visible beside the bed. Fear got a hold of her, and she screamed. He grabbed the bed with one hand, sending it flying across the room. He reached down, caught the terrified woman by the hair dragging her to her feet, and with one swipe of his mighty hand, slapped her so hard across the face he knocked her out.

It took half an hour before she regained consciousness, to find herself bound and gagged in a chair. Harry towered over her; his disfigured face made her shiver. He removed the towel from her mouth and she screamed:

"Someone help me," she yelled with tears in her eyes.

The saw roared, his mangled hands holding it right in front of her. Her eyes widened with horror.

"What do you want from me? Who are you?" she sobbed.

The chainsaw fell silent.

"Who am I? Do you remember this?" he barked holding the gold ring in front of her.

"My God Harry?" She asked confused.

"You left me for this?" He screamed, holding the dead man's head in front of her.

She turned pale. He threw the man's head across the room.

"Harry, I'm sorry, I--" that was far as she got before the saw screamed to life again to cut her short.

"Now you die," he yelled, pushing the blade through her stomach.

She had been cut in half right up the middle her split body dangling either side of the chair.

He walked off into the night a nasty grin on his face, tossing the ring into the flowerbed, before disappearing into the shadows. He had made those that had humiliated him suffer, but he has a taste for murder now and he likes it. This maniac will not stop for anything. Pain and suffering will follow wherever he goes.

As he strolled through the night a black cloud of smoke appeared before him and the man in black materialized from the smoke smiling.

"Well done Harry you have surpassed my expectations. I see you have had your revenge but there are four people that I want you to destroy. Look carefully at this my soul harvester," the man opened his palm and a grey smoke rose and within the smoke faces began to appear that of Jackie, Sarah, Roger and Ben.

"These four must be destroyed Harry before I can begin my plans of world domination, kill them and there will be great rewards bestowed upon you but fail me and your suffering will be eternal," he vanished in another cloud of smoke and Gordon's chest heaved and fell as he felt the rage once more, his eyes burned red and he continued on his way.

*At the Aces High:*

Ben, Jackie, Roger, and Sarah had bumped into two of their friends, Will Jackson and Laura Jennings. They were sitting round talking and drinking to Ben and Jackie's engagement. They were drunk and laughing.

"You know, we've always known you two would do this one day and I'm thrilled for you both," Will said, while he raised his glass to finish his drink, then pounded the glass back on the table and burped.

Will worked in the same factory as Ben and he was a big guy. He stood at least six foot two and into bodybuilding. The man was big. Laura Jennings was his fiancée of two years. She was a night school teacher, teaching adult Spanish and German. They left the nightclub together, staggering off down the street.

"I can't believe I'm marrying the most beautiful woman on the planet," Ben said giving Jackie a kiss on the cheek.

"Will you stop," she said with a giggle.

As they turned onto the gloomy lane, a chainsaw roared in the woods beside them. They looked at each other; Ben held Jackie's hand tight.

"What was that?" Laura asked trembling.

Suddenly, a huge chainsaw wielding man emerged from the wooded area standing in front of them, an evil grin on his mutilated face. He was revving the engine and laughing.

"Look at the size of that guy. He's huge," Roger said, looking at Sarah, whose eyes were fixed on the menacing character in front of them.

"What do you want freak?" Will shouted clenching his fists.

Harry laughed disappearing back into the shadows.

"Let's make a run for it. If we make it to my house, we can call for help," Sarah yelled, running past where the man had vanished.

He watched them running, laughing to himself as they all ran past him. He watched them disappear around a bend.

He ran through the woods following them. They were out of breath, panting heavy by the time they got to Sarah's.

"What or, who was that?" Laura asked, holding onto Will.

"Who or whatever it was, it's fucking big," Roger added, slamming the door and bolting it.

Sarah picked up the phone to call for help, but instead of a dial tone, she heard nothing. The line was dead. She slammed the receiver

"Damn phone's dead," she yelled.

Just then, the chainsaw started again.

"What does he want from us?" Laura screamed placing her hands over her ears.

The chainsaw roared as it cut through the door. With a hard kick the door shattered, Harry stood there breathing hard, rage running through him.

"Who the hell are you?" Will growled with anger in his eyes.

"Oh! Where are my manners? Harry Gordon's the name and murder is the game. Do you want to play?" He said with a ghastly smile the chainsaw humming and spluttering.

"I'll kill you," Will barked running at Gordon trying to get the chainsaw from him.

Big as Will was, he was no match for Harry's psychotic rage. He pushed Will against the wall, the blade cutting across his body through his stomach. Will screamed in terrifying agony.

"No. Will," Laura, yelled, Sarah and Jackie held her back.

"Into the basement quick," Sarah ordered.

Jackie looked behind, and there was Gordon coming straight at her with the saw roaring. Her eyes opened wide with terror. Just as the death blade was about to cut into her, Ben stepped in front of her, screaming as it cut his chest. He fell to the ground, curled into a ball in severe pain, blood soaking through his jacket. Jackie watched in horror as Gordon towered over him laughing.

"Ben," she bellowed with tears in her eyes.

Gordon looked at her, then back at Ben. He lay there with his hands covered in blood, his breathing becoming shallow and laboured.

Gordon bent over with the saw still humming.

"Oh! Don't you worry Ben, you won't be dying alone. I will take that fine-looking woman of yours and put her beside you in little bitty pieces. In fact, I will kill all of you," he said standing moving toward the basement.

The others had run to the basement and locked the door. Jackie could feel tears in her eyes, the horrible sound of the evil machine ringing through her mind. They heard heavy footsteps coming down the hallway and the humming of the chainsaw engine. The motor roared, and the door shattered. Laura screamed as Harry came bounding in. He found the light switch and grabbed a hold of her throwing her to the ground. He arched the chainsaw over his head swinging it downward on a terrified Laura when Jackie crept up behind him.

"Get away from her you bastard," she yelled, jumping on his back, clawing at his face and eyes.

He bent over sending her crashing to the ground with such power she blacked out.

"I'll save you for last bitch," he growled, turning his attention back to Laura.

*Up in the living room:*

Ben climbed to his feet and wobbled toward the basement. He heard the saws roaring engine and Laura's screams of terror. He staggered down the stairs. When he reached the last step, he could see Harry holding the saw above Laura's legs. He took a deep breath and felt his anger rise. Harry had his back to him so didn't notice him. Ben rushed at Gordon with a shoulder tackle knocking him off Laura. Ben was sick from the shock and loss of blood. Jackie regained consciousness, and got to her feet and was relieved to see Ben standing there.

Harry came at them again Roger and Sarah stepped up beside Ben and Jackie.

Laura curled up in a frightened ball in the corner. Harry laughed revving the engine walking toward them. Ben and Roger walked to his right side, making sure they got his attention. Suddenly, he charged at them swinging the saw everywhere trying to trap them in a corner.

"Roger, break left," Ben yelled, as he staggered to Gordon's right.

Harry was after Ben.

"You're finished now boy," He screamed forcing Ben into a corner. Roger crept up behind Gordon with a baseball bat he had found in a storage box. He took a deep breath and lashed out at Gordon with everything he had. There was an enormous crack as the bat connected with Harry's skull. Gordon turned to face Roger.

"So, you want to play rough do ya? I'll show you rough," Gordon screamed, running toward Roger swinging the blade in a blinding arc.

Roger dropped the bat, and Ben picked it up from the floor. Jackie and Sarah had found golf clubs. Ben attacked first belting the bat into Gordon as hard as he could. Gordon was dazed as he turned to Ben. Jackie whacked the golf club into Harry's left knee and Sarah hit him in the right knee, he dropped to the floor. He roared raising the saw above his head. Ben drew back the baseball bat and mangled Gordon's right hand. The chainsaw fell from his grip and Jackie seized it with both hands. Harry stood again grabbing Ben by the throat with his left hand.

"You can never win," he growled squeezing, choking the life out of him.

Jackie saw the opportunity and ran up behind Gordon the motor revving ripping his back open. Harry screamed releasing Ben, his hands trying to clutch his torn back. Sarah and Roger attacked with the golf clubs at the same time sending Harry staggering backwards, blood squirting from his head, he fell against the wall sliding to the floor in a daze. He tried to grab Jackie's leg, but she used the saw and cut off his arm just above the elbow.

He roared in agony. She revved the engine again and kept cutting into him until he was nothing more than a pile of severed parts. Blood splattered her face; she dropped the machine and cried.

Roger and Sarah helped Ben and Laura into the sitting room. Sarah ran for five minutes to Jackie's calling for help. Ben's breathing was shallow now, and Jackie sat holding him with tears in her eyes.

In the basement the remains of Harry lay scattered on the floor right beside the blood-stained chainsaw. Without warning, an intense light beamed from the blade surrounding the dismembered body. Piece by piece he was being reassembled by an unexplainable evil force. After a few minutes, his entire body was fully regenerated. The blinding light vanished, and he lay there. Suddenly, he stretched out one of his arms towards the sky gasping for breath. He sat upright, looked around him, smiling. His huge hand picked up the saw, and he stood. Sirens were echoing in the distance; he hid in the darkest corner.

Paramedics and police arrived. Ben was being looked after, he had a nasty cut across his chest, and it would need many stitches.

Meanwhile, Laura was so traumatized she couldn't even talk. Roger, Jackie, and Sarah walked beside Ben as they wheeled him out on a stretcher, to the ambulance; another stretcher emerged from the house. It was Will; he was barely alive, but alive nonetheless.

At the hospital, they sat in the waiting room while doctors looked after Ben. The door opened and two cops approached them. They told the officers what had happened, and it was then the cops told them that the man who attacked them was the same man responsible for sixty brutal murders.

"And what are you going to do with his body?" Sarah asked with a stern look on her face.

One cop looked at her confused and spoke.

"What body are you talking about?"

"The one in the basement, He's in pieces. We killed him," Jackie barked.

"I'm sorry but I don't know what you're talking about. We've just finished searching the house and there's nothing there," the cop said with a puzzled look on his face.

Back at the house, police were finishing another search of the basement when Harry crept from his hiding place. The saw roared, and the screaming began again. He walked from the house into the woods.

He looked back, and laughed, raising the chainsaw high above his head screaming, "You can't kill me. I'll be back," then he disappeared into the woods.

He is the harvester of souls and death is what he lives for.

# DARK REFLECTIONS

Two weeks have passed since their battle with Harry Gordon, in which one of our heroes ended up in the hospital. Ben was coming home today after receiving over eighty stitches to his chest where the chainsaw had cut him, and Will was fortunate to be alive. It took surgeons over ten hours to put him back together again. However, there was a noticeable change in Will's attitude, an evil nasty change. The devil gave Gordon a saw that was forged in the fires of hell from a metal not found anywhere in this world. It came from the dark side of the moon, and once every four years for two nights, the dark side shines down upon us, and not only does the saw give Harry immortality it does something else. Because of its evil origins, the metal of the saw will resurrect those who have died from Gordon's rage turning them into marauding demons, and those injured by the saw will suffer a similar fate depending on how badly they have been injured.

Tonight, the dark side will face the Earth for two nights, and those who have died will rise again. Harry killed over sixty people, and tonight they will rise and converge on Los Angeles, for one purpose: To kill whoever stands in their way. They will tear limb from body and flesh from bone, anyone unfortunate enough to encounter their savagery will be slaughtered, but soon after, they will be resurrected as bloodthirsty killers, joining the unholy legion of the undead, and they in turn will kill and spill innocent blood.

This had happened before, two hundred thirty years ago; Harry Gordon isn't the devils first soul collector, but the second. Kenneth Bronson was the first, and he slaughtered people in the hundreds. Not with a chainsaw, but a powerful sword he wielded high above his head, as he cut and chopped his way through villages.

Men, women, and children fell under the flashing blade as log cabins burned and people ran screaming. Four years after this blood bath, the dead rose from their graves one stormy night, going on a brutal murderous rampage. The survivors barricaded themselves inside an old monastery while, outside, demons pounded and hammered the heavy wooden gates trying to break it down.

In the monastery, the monks busily constructed something, a mystical mirror. For nine hours they worked, polishing the glass, making the frame from gold and silver. When they finished the Abbot appeared with a huge book, flipped through the leaves to a page, then raising his hands above his head and gazing to the heavens, he chanted in Latin. As he spoke, the mirror levitated toward the ceiling. A red glow surrounded the mystical glass, and it spun round and round, faster and faster. The Abbot was still chanting and the other monks looked at each other in both fear and awe. Without warning, a brilliant white flash came from the mirror's glass. It lit up the whole room so bright the monks shielded their eyes from the blinding glow. The Abbot stopped chanting, and the glow disappeared, the mirror floated to the ground, standing there as if it was being held up by the divine hand of God.

"Come my brothers bring the mirror. I pray we are not too late," The Abbot cried, running up the twisting stairway.

Two monks carried the mirror and were straining under the weight. They climbed another set of steps that brought them to the top wall. They propped the mirror against the wall and looked down to see the demons had surrounded them.

"Put the mirror here hurry," the Abbot ordered. The two monks groaned lifting the mirror.

The Abbot raised his hands, speaking in Latin once more. The mirror levitated, dropping down to the demons, hovering four feet from the ground. The demons could see themselves, and they screamed and hissed at their reflections. They raised their arms across their eyes, seeing their hideous deformed faces in the glass. The Abbot raised his voice, and the mirror glowed. The demons stepped back, moaning and hissing as it floated into the air, and spun. They were frozen to the spot until the same blinding flash shot from the glass. The dominions of hell screamed as one by one the mirror pulled them into the black spiralling vortex. Faster and faster, it spun. For half an hour, the demons screamed, disappearing into the void. No matter where they tried to hide, they were dragged from their hiding places; as if something was lifting them into the air, casting them into the mirrored vortex, into a black abyss where nightmares and evil dwell. They sunk their clawed fingers into the ground as they were vacuumed, screaming toward the glass, their fingers tearing channels into the clay. The last demon vanished into the mirror. It stopped spinning, turned on its back with the glass pointing to the heavens. A bright red light beamed into the midnight sky as the evil was expelled back to the dark side. Demons flew from the mirror at light speed, a never-ending stream of evil twisted faces. When the last of the evil was cast back to hell, the mirror floated back to the ground, landing upright, before it wobbled back and forth falling down lying there. It was over at least for now.

That was two hundred thirty years ago. After that night, the mirror was hidden never to be found.

Tonight, Harry's victims will live again. Tonight, will be hell on earth!

Jackie, Roger, Sarah, and Laura were at the hospital in the waiting room. There was a buzz of excitement in the air, and Jackie just couldn't sit still. She stood, pacing back and forth.

"Will you try to relax," Sarah said with a gentle smile.

Jackie looked at her as the door opened, and in walked a doctor. He was holding a folder in his left hand and a pen in the other. The big thick glasses he wore hid his eyes, and he smiled.

"Well, how is he?" Jackie asked with a nervous tremor in her voice.

"Why don't you ask him yourself?" the doctor said, opening the door.

Ben walked in with a huge smile.

"So, did you miss me?" Jackie threw her arms around him kissing him.

Sarah ran and hugged him; Roger waited his turn and just shook his hand.

"Welcome back mate. It wasn't the same without you."

"I know I've missed you too." He stopped and looked at Laura who was crying.

He looked at the doctor and asked

"How is Will doc?" They waited with suppressed apprehension for the doctor's response. A serious expression appeared on the doctor's face. He adjusted his glasses, clearing his throat. Laura went pale, Jackie and Sarah stood beside her, placing their arms around her. The doctor took a deep breath

"The injuries that Mr. Jackson received were serious. We had to remove part of the large intestine, one of his kidneys and part of his liver. He is fortunate to be alive, if he had been cut just a centimetre lower, he would undoubtedly have died. I'm afraid he will have a nasty scar for the rest of his days," The doctor stopped as he saw a saddened, sorrowful look appear across their faces.

"An injury like that should have killed him, that he is still alive is a miracle. He has healed remarkably fast, which is unheard of, with this kind of injury and I have not seen anything like it in my years as a practising physician. He can go home today, but he must do nothing too strenuous. He needs rest and plenty of it. I don't see why he should not make a full recovery in time. Now if you will excuse me, I'll arrange for your discharge."

The group were stunned into silence as the doctor left. Laura was pleased that Will was going home with them until they met him in the corridor by the main reception desk.

Ben had just signed his discharge papers when Will was pushed up in a wheelchair.

"Will," Laura, screamed in an over excited tone.

She ran up to him, bending over to kiss him.

"Get away from me," he roared pushing her backward. She fell to the ground, stunned and shocked.

"What, the hell is wrong with you?" Roger barked helping Laura to her feet.

She was in tears. Will looked pale and drained, with big black circles under his eyes.

"HA! HA! HA!" he laughed and rose from the wheelchair.

"Oh, look at me, I'm little miss perfect. You're nothing but a dumb blonde bitch," Will yelled at her.

Jackie and Sarah were shocked; they looked at each other, mouths open to say something but just couldn't find the words.

"What are you looking at?" He barked staring at Jackie.

Ben lost his cool. He grabbed Will by the collar, pushing him back in the wheelchair.

"Now you listen to me, you son of a bitch. I don't care how injured you are or what the hell has come over you. But I'm warning you. If you ever talk to Laura, Jackie, or Sarah that way again, I swear I'll put you in this wheelchair permanently. You got that," Ben growled.

Will just laughed an evil laugh, pushing Ben away from him.

"You're pathetic," he yelled, standing up again.

"What are you looking at geek?" he pushed Roger.

Roger clenched his fist, and punched him in the face, knocking him to the ground. Will sat up spitting out blood laughing. Security personnel arrived to bring calm to the madness, restraining Will who was getting out of hand again.

"Let's go Rodge. He's not himself. Let's get out of here," Ben said, placing his hand on Roger's shoulder.

They turned around to leave, and were just at the main doors when Will screamed,

"You're all going to die," his laughter faded as they walked out the doors into the car park.

Jackie drove the Mustang, as Ben was still too weak, and in pain. He sat beside her with the others in the back, glancing in the rear-view mirror he saw Laura with tears streaming from her eyes. He shook his head in disgust.

"Jackie, can you pull the car over please? I'm not feeling so good," he said swallowing hard.

He sat on the hood with Jackie beside him, his hand across his chest. His face had an agonizing look across it and he moaned, bending forward. Jackie's face filled with concern.

"Are you O.K. Ben?" She asked putting her arm around his shoulders.

"I feel like I've been hit by a freight train," he rested his head on her shoulder as she held him.

A strange feeling came over him.

"What's wrong?" She asked, as she felt him shivering.

His eyes opened wide sitting upright.

"I don't fucking know what's wrong OK!" he screamed. Jackie was startled by his outburst.

"Jackie I'm sorry. For a minute there, I had this weird cold feeling run through me, and this cut sent extreme pain through my body. It felt like I was someone else. I'm sorry baby," his arms trembled as he put them around her, holding her tight.

His mind wandered for a second.

*"Will was nearly killed by Gordon, and you saw what's happening to him. I was only moderately injured and I'm acting strange and crazy. Could this have something to do with Gordon and that damn saw?"* He pondered before he spoke.

"My wound is driving me crazy, and I got hit in the chest. Will was hurt worse than me and look what happened to him. He's turned evil now," Ben stopped and thought for a second.

"What are you saying Ben?" Jackie looked concerned.

"What if this has something to do with Gordon and his damn

chainsaw? Will and I got hurt badly with it, now look at him and me," Ben clutched at his chest again.

The pain was unreal. He gagged and held back from vomiting.

Time was ticking on, in four short hours the sun would be setting in L.A. The dark side of the moon was coming into alignment with the Earth, and hell is about to break loose.

In Alaska, the last rays of the sun turned the sky a red-orange colour. Birds flew home to roost, and the nocturnal creatures began their nightly quest for food. At the logging site, which had been shut down after Harry, slaughtered everyone, all seemed quiet.

A small graveyard stood at the rear of the site where twenty-nine graves lay side by side. A grey wolf appeared on the edge of the graveyard sniffing at the air. The hair stood on its back and it growled, baring its teeth. The wolf barked and growled low in its throat repeatedly for a while before it whimpered and ran away. Frightened birds took flight from the trees, and a howling wind echoed through the campsite the wooden crosses that marked the graves shook and tilted.

Then it happened.

Half-decaying hands shot up from the graves, decaying twisted mutilated bodies rose from their resting place. They moaned the song of the damned as they shuffled along following some invisible force. Their rotting limbs making each step a jerky struggle.

Their skin was ashen, smoke grey, eyes yellow and penetrating, their teeth pointed and serrated, hands with long fingers lined with razor-sharp nails. They were driven by an invisible force, an uncontrollable want to keep moving into the night. Twenty-nine demons marched through the woods where they had died, stopping outside the cave where Harry received the chainsaw three weeks earlier. A dark figure emerged from the cave and the demons hissed and scratched at the air.

"Easy my children, I have summoned you back to the land of the living for a purpose," The man in black spoke from the shadows.

"Come now. Follow me through here," With a wave of his hand a vortex opened. It was a gateway.

The man stepped through it, and one by one, the demons followed.

Will was transforming. He lay on his bed, shivering and shaking as if he had been in a freezer for hours. His hair had fallen out; his skin turned to a deathly ashen grey. His body was filled with pain, he screamed, as his fingers grew longer. Skin stretched tighter, making bones crack, and twisted claws grew from his fingertips, ripping out his fingernails. He sat upright in the bed, breathing incredibly fast; a cold sweat dappled his brow. He put his arms around himself and shivered again.

His eyes burned, he rubbed them with his hands, but his new claws ripped gouges in his skin. He gasped for breath falling back on his bed, lifeless. For a time, he lay there motionless, when, without warning, he sat upright, and screamed a terrible scream that sounded like a hissing snake and tortured feline. His eyes were luminous in the dark as they burned with evil. The transformation was complete.

*Back at Laura's house:*

They were sitting talking and drinking coffee. Jackie and Sarah wanted to stay with Laura after the day's earlier events left her shaken. After half an hour, Ben and Roger left.

"Jackie. Here are the car keys. I need to get some fresh air and Roger is coming with me," he kissed her placing the keys in her hand.

"I'm staying with Jackie, Roger. I'll be home later, okay," Sarah kissed him at the front door.

"Okay my love," Roger replied, dipping his hands in his leather jacket pockets.

"It's freezing tonight," he said, blowing his hot breath steaming into the cold air as they both walked at a quick pace.

As they passed by Will's house, they could hear frightened screams coming from within.

"This is not good," Ben whispered as he and Roger ran to the back window and looked inside.

*Somewhere over the far side of town:*

A vortex appeared and demons poured out, a blood-red moon appearing from behind the clouds. The shadowy figure emerged soon after and laughed.

"Now, my children go forth and destroy. I have seen the future. The four must die if my plans are to succeed. Find them my children and tear them apart," He yelled, raising his hands over his head, his eyes burning red.

The demons growled, showing their sharp teeth, and marched into the darkness.

*Back over at the Jackson residence:*

Ben and Roger were shocked by what they were seeing.

"What the hell is that?" Roger asked, confused looking through the window.

Will's father lay on the floor in a pool of blood, teeth marks on his face and neck, where chunks of flesh had been ripped out. The demon was now attacking his mother, and she was trying to fight him. She pushed him away as he tried to bite and get his claws on her. She dug her fingernails into its face, tearing deep gouges into its icy flesh, strips of skin dangling from her nails. When she fought back, it grabbed her by the shoulder sinking its teeth deep into her neck. She screamed as she began to decay, her body wrinkling up and shrivelling as life was being drained from her. The dried-up skin peeled open, and her eyes looked like dried up prunes. Her withered body fell to the floor, and the demon towered over it. It turned around as the back door was kicked open. There, stood Ben and Roger. The demon snarled and growled, looking at them with eyes so evil; they could burn a hole right through you. It charged at Ben pinning him to the wall. He struggled to get free when Roger hit it from behind, releasing Ben, it went after Roger. It got hold of him by the throat and pinned him to the kitchen table. Roger gasped for breath as the demon's eyes glowed. They had seen what it did to Will's mother. Ben jumped on its back trying to make it release Roger, its strength was unreal. Ben got off its back, went to its left side, and punched it again and again in the face. It had no effect. Suddenly, it released Roger as it looked out the window. It could hear the other demons approaching; it screamed, walking off into the night.

"Holy shit, what the hell was that thing?" Roger said getting his breath back

"A God dam demon Rodge, fuck we have to go back to the girls now," Ben yelled, both of them running out through the door.

As they ran back down the street, they were confronted by more demons. Out of the night they came, hissing, and moaning, their arms out stretched, ready for the kill. They were surrounded.

"Where the hell did, they come out of?" Roger barked, looking around at the evil beings closing in around them.

"Fuck! We're surrounded. We have to get around them," Ben, replied, his fists clenched.

The demons were so close now they were within touching distance. Ben saw an opening appear between the demons.

"Run for it," he screamed as they both ran past the creatures, who tried to catch them as they went by.

Ten minutes later, they arrived back at Laura's out of breath. They pounded on the door and Laura opened it. They bolted inside, slamming the door shut. Laura looked at them puzzled.

"What's going on with you two?" She asked. She shrugged her shoulders and went to the kitchen while the others walked to the sitting room.

"God, what's up with you two?" Sarah asked, as Ben and Roger looked at each other.

"The whole town is crawling with demons," Roger told the story, when a loud bang came from the kitchen, followed by Laura's high-pitched scream.

They ran to the kitchen and saw Laura being dragged by the hair through the back door by a demon. Roger grabbed a knife from the table and slashed the demon's hands. It released her, and she ran to Sarah. Roger swung the knife, the blade connecting with the demon's throat, sending yellow blood gushing to the floor. The demon clutched its injured throat as blood dribbled between the fingers. He stabbed the creature three times in the chest, and it fell to the ground dead. He dragged the body outside and ran back locking the door. Ben's car was gone, so was Jackie.

"Jesus, I forgot Jackie. Where is she?" Ben asked.

"She took the car, said she was going home to get a few things," Sarah said realizing her best friend was in serious danger.

"Where's the phone?" Ben asked going into the sitting room.

He dialled and waited. The phone rang but there was no answer.

"Come on Jackie pick up," he whispered to himself.

"There's no answer, I'm going over there," he said running to the back door.

He was reaching out his hand to open it, when he grimaced and went pale. Agony ran through him, and he clutched his chest.

"Are you alright?" Roger asked, coming to his side.

"Don't worry about me. I'll be fine. You stay here and watch the girls," He took off into the night.

As he ran, the pain in his chest hit him again, worse this time, and he fell to the ground writhing in agony with tears in his eyes. He didn't see the demons coming around the corner as he lay there curled up in a ball clutching his chest.

He heard them moan as they moved in for the kill. They shuffled toward him, their moaning, and hissing getting more intense as they were on top of him now. He looked up and saw ten creatures closing in on him "Oh shit," He groaned trying to get to his feet. There were only ten demons, but Ben was in no condition to fight now as he dropped on his back breathing heavy. They closed in for the kill.

"I love you Jackie," He whispered as they pounced on him.

*Over at Jackie's:*

The Mustang pulled into the driveway. She got out and walked to the front door. As soon as she was inside, she locked it, placing the security chain across it.

"May as well get a shower while I'm here," she said to herself putting the keys on the phone desk in the hall.

She missed the little red light blinking on her answering machine.

The demons were all over Ben, and he was trying hard to fight them back. Roger came charging around the corner with an axe gripped in his hands. He ran to help his friend that was in serious trouble. He raised the axe high above his head and smashed a demon's head open.

"That's my best friend you're messing with, you mess with him, then you have to mess with me," He grinned as the demons turned their attention to him.

The axe slashed through the air, and another demon met its demise.

The pain left Ben; he sat upright, and staggered to his feet. He walked up behind a demon, caught it by the head, twisting it to the left producing a snap as its neck broke. Roger swung the axe again, and another demon fell to the ground. Ben went nuts, punching, and kicking everything that stood in his way. The last body dropped dead. He looked at Roger and smiled

"Thanks, Rodge. I owe you one. Are the girls alright?" He asked catching his breath.

"Who do you think told me to come after you?" Roger replied putting the axe down by his side.

Ben was pale and shaking.

"Ben you're in no condition to go alone, I'm coming with you,"

Roger walked beside him.

"I thought you might," Ben replied as they moved onward.

They took the shortcut to Jackie's house through a small wood at the back. They ran to the front door and could hear a radio upstairs. Ben pounded on the door;

"Jackie, it's me," He yelled, but she couldn't hear with the music.

"We have to go in the back door," he said, moving around to the rear of the house.

He stood on an old steel barrel, fumbling around in the guttering for the spare back door key.

"I got it," he said, climbing from the barrel.

They went inside, and could hear the water running and Jackie was humming to herself,

"Jackie! Are you alright?" Ben called out up the stairs.

The water stopped, and the radio went silent, then she appeared at the top of the landing wrapped in a bath towel. She gazed at the two guys looking puzzled.

"I'm fine. Why are the two of you here?" She stopped as a loud bang came from the front door frightening them.

Roger sauntered to the front room, pulled back the curtain and peeped out.

"Fuck! They're here," He whispered, running back to the others.

"Jackie. Get dressed now. We have to go," Ben ran up the stairs to her side and took her to the bedroom.

"Ben what's wrong?" She asked, letting the towel slip to the floor, her wet naked body glistening in the bedroom light.

"The whole town is over run by demons. God knows where they came from but they're here," he explained, while Jackie slipped into a pair of jeans, and a T-shirt. Then Roger burst into the room,

"We've got to go now, the door won't hold up much longer," he said with fear written over his face. Jackie slipped on her shoes and they ran down the stairs, just as they reached the last step the front door flew open, and demons in the hundreds poured in on top of them.

"Holy shit head for the back door," Jackie screamed as they headed for the kitchen.

Ben forgot to lock it; they opened it and ran to the little wooded area that took them out onto the streets. The demons were shuffling after them when they reached the wooded area; they smelled the air and screamed. They dragged their decaying bodies through the woods in pursuit.

Ben, Jackie, and Roger were just running past the old cemetery when something bright shone in the distance. They approached the glowing object cautiously. Something protruded from the ground half buried. Roger was not impressed at their discovery.

"Just a stupid old mirror," He exclaimed with a disappointing tone.

Ben got on his knees to have a closer look at it then he dug round the mirror with his hands. Inside the hole he made was a book; he reached in, pulled it out and opened it. He read a few pages to himself, and then looked up at the others.

"What is it?" Jackie asked.

"Over two hundred years ago the mirror was constructed by a group of monks after demons over ran the town. We have a weapon," he showed them the book.

Roger and Jackie were reading it while Ben continued the digging for the mirror. Placing his hands on the edges he pulled hard, but it didn't move.

"Roger, give me a hand with this. It weighs a ton," he said while trying it again. They both pulled with all their might.

The mirror came free, and they carried it, taking little breaks in between to catch their breath. They reached Laura's house. Sarah had seen them coming in the gate and opened the door for them.

"What the hell is that?" She asked in a serious tone closing the door.

"No time to explain now," Ben said as he and Roger rushed by her to the sitting room laying the mirror against the wall.

They stood there looking at it, wondering how the hell a mirror would save them from this evil. Jackie read the book, and everyone focused. She told of how the Abbot and his monks built the mirror, and what it had done to the demons. It told of a mystical blade that started all of this, the sword of Kenneth Bronson.

"What if that chainsaw is made of the same metal?" Sarah asked

"It could be how this is happening," she continued. The others nodded their heads in agreement.

Jackie kept reading. For five minutes she read until she came to the end.

"If you are reading this journal,then the mirror has revealed its hiding place, and I fear that evil has once again reared its ugly head. This mirror may only come to life with a sacred, ancient, Latin text the passage is written in this book. You must speak the words precisely, for just as the mirror can destroy the demons, so too can it destroy you. Speak the words and let the mirrors, light bring an end to the darkness. When the creatures of darkness are trapped in the mirror, it will send them back to where they first came, to the dark side of the moon. I pray you will be victorious; may God protect you on your quest. These are the last words of Brother Marcus Seville. Dated August 17, 1766," Jackie closed the book and sat beside Ben.

"Oh great, who here can speak Latin?" Roger stood up kicking his empty beer can across the floor.

His anger was understandable. They were arguing amongst themselves when a huge bang at the door made them jump.

"What the hell was that?" Sarah ran to the window.

She pulled back the curtain and screamed as hundreds of demons stared right back at her.

"Upstairs now," Ben shouted as they ran, leaving the mirror behind them.

They ran to Laura's bedroom, locking the door. Below they could hear glass shatter, as the demons broke through the windows.

"Fuck! We forgot the mirror," Ben screamed hammering his fist off the door.

"We still have the book," Jackie said with a grin.

They could hear the demons coming up the stairs; their moans sent shivers down their spines.

"Jackie I'm frightened," Laura said with terror in her eyes. Jackie placed her arm around her.

The monk's journal lay on the bed, and the pages turned over by themselves. The gang stood there mesmerized by what they were seeing. Suddenly, a ghostly figure appeared and smiled. It was a monk. He picked up the book disappearing through the closed door.

"What was that?" Roger exclaimed, looking at Ben.

Ben was going to reply when a loud voice speaking in Latin came through the door. The demons screamed, and hissed, as the voice continued getting louder and louder, something or someone was translating the text.

They could hear the demons shuffling back down the stairs, and the voice still bellowing. Ben unlocked the door and peeped out; the demons were gone. Roger, Sarah, Jackie, and Laura appeared at the top of the stairs beside him. As they crept down the stairs, through the sitting room window, a blinding glow appeared, and the demons, now outside, screamed. The mirror was working, and they were being dragged into it.

They ran to the front door, looked out, and there was the mirror floating in mid-air, spinning round and round at amazing speed. It was a vacuum sucking the demons back. They screamed and hissed as they disappeared into the mirrors glass. For the next ten minutes, demons vanished into this mirror of magic, until the last evil creature vanished into the black vortex. The mirror turned over and pointed the glass to the sky. A red glow appeared, and demons flew from it at light speed, a never-ending stream of evil twisted faces. The mirror spun again, and the monk reappeared. He waved at the gang and smiled before both he and the mirror disappeared forever.

"Did you see that? What just happened" Laura asked with a wobble in her voice.

"I don't know, but it's over now," Sarah put her arm around Laura, hugging her.

"No. It's not over yet. That chainsaw is made of that metal and it won't stop until it and Harry Gordon are both destroyed," Ben said, lighting up a smoke, and they went back inside to clean up the mess.

Somewhere in the desert wasteland, a light flickered inside a cave. It's a campfire and sitting there was Harry Gordon. His mutilated twisted face grinning as he polished his precious saw. His reflection shone in the gleaming silver, and he yelled. It reminded him of what Jackie had done to him, of how she used his own weapon against him and he whispered to himself;

"I'll get you bitch. If it's the last thing I do, I'll get you, and I'll show you the true meaning of the word pain," he growled.

The memory of Jackie was strong in his mind, her death and the death of the others was all he cared for now.

"I'll send you to hell, and you'll be screaming all the way," he yelled, the saw roaring into the night, and then his laughter echoed through the darkness.

"I'll kill you bitch," He screamed as he cut through the rocks sending sparks flying in every direction.

The four survivors of his rage better watch out, because the chainsaw will roar again, and the body count will rise. Harry's machine is hungry for blood, he is hungry for revenge, and his vengeance will not be quick and painless....

# RISE OF THE FOUR

## TERROR AT DEVIL'S MANSION

Many years ago, just on the outskirts of the city, there lived an old man with his twenty-four-year-old daughter. He was a scientist and Archaeologist, obsessed with eternal youth, and immortality. One day, he left for Egypt on a six-month archaeological expedition. While there, he discovered a book, buried in a pyramid he picked it up and read through it; a huge grin appeared on his face, and he hid the book in his suitcase. He studied the book night after night until his return to America.

Upon his arrival home, Charles Bradford set to work at once setting up his laboratory, spending days upon days mixing formulas, and translating the ancient Egyptian text. He worked continuously for over a month, and then finally, he cracked the code and laughed. He mixed liquids together Red, green; yellow and blue all in a vial. He spoke the words from the book; the liquid bubbled and change colour. A dark red vapour appeared in the vial drifting across the table. The liquid turned a bright gold colour then to black. He took a syringe, filled it with the liquid then held up the needle, and squirted a little fluid from the hollow point. Walking over to another table where four white rats scurried around in a cage. He reached in his hand and picked one out, the rat squealed when his hand clamped around its body.

"Easy now, this won't hurt," he whispered, inserting the needle, and injecting the serum. He placed the rat back in the cage with the others, watched and waited.

The infected rat lay there twitching, and squealing, when the serum took its effect. The rodent increased in size, teeth growing longer along with its claws. Charles frowned as his new creation destroyed the other rats. His pet ripped the others to pieces, and ear-piercing squeals filled the room, but he was not happy. The formula was supposed to give immortality, not create a monster. He had a loaded pistol in his desk drawer, and when he was sliding the drawer out a terrible squeaking, creaking noise came from the cage. His hand trembled, his fingers curled around the pistol, he ran back to the cage. His eyes opened in amazement when he gazed inside, stunned at what he saw. The infected rat had grown to triple its original size. In a rage, Charles pointed the gun at the rat and fired.

It lay dead, shot in the head. He lowered the gun, walking back to his desk and dropped it with a thud. Standing over the book reading line by line trying to find what went wrong. He was concentrating hard when a sudden noise made him jump. He looked around the room, but there was nothing, then his attention shifted to the cage. Cautiously he walked over to it, hearing the cage rattle, and when he gazed inside, he stumbled backward in shock. The rat he had shot was alive again, trying to move in the limited space in the confines of its prison. Charles trembled, his eyes fixed on this thing he had created, eyes snow-white, hair grown so much it looked like a miniature lion with teeth, claws and viciousness to match.

"Good, God in Heaven what have I created?" He asked himself running his fingers through his matted grey hair.

While he concentrated on the rodent, Charles never heard his daughter enter the room. From the shadows, she watched him holding a syringe, and then a terrible squealing pierced through her ears. She moved closer until she stood right behind her father. She screamed when she saw the rat. Charles turned around, startled by her scream, still holding the syringe. When he turned around, the needle jabbed Elizabeth in the arm, he stood back in terror when he realized what he'd done.

"Elizabeth, my dear Elizabeth. What have I done?" He said backing away from her with tears in his eyes. She looked at him pulling out the needle.

"I am fine father, it's just a scratch," she said with a smile, showing him the little puncture mark on her arm.

Charles fell backward, clutching his chest, gasping for breath.

"Father," Elizabeth screamed.

He tumbled to the ground, knocking vials of liquid and test tubes over, and they shattered on the floor. She ran to his side, kneeling down beside him. She cradled him in her arms; His breathing became weak, and shallow. Charles looked up at his daughter with his grey, blue, eyes.

"My darling Elizabeth, what have I done to you, my daughter? I have been a fool to meddle with things beyond my comprehension. When one grows old, the questions of one's own mortality come to mind. Death comes to us all, my dear Elizabeth and death scared me, so I wanted to find a way to live for longer. But I know now, that death is a part of life that we all must face, because time eventually runs out for us all. I'm sorry my dear Elizabeth," he stopped talking, gasping for breath.

He reached out, caressing his daughter's cheek, before his arm dropped to the floor with a heavy thump. His breathing slowed to a whisper; his eyes fixed on his distraught daughter. His breathing slowed, and his heart stopped. Charles was dead.

She cried, holding him in her arms, her dark green eyes, and long, flowing, brown hair wet with tears. Suddenly, her mouth opened wide as if she was choking on something.

She dropped her dead father to the floor, clutching at her throat. She could not breathe, getting to her feet in a panic, crashing into bookcases and against walls fighting to catch her breath. She felt an incredible pain throughout her body; the serum was taking effect beginning a terrifying transformation changing her from human to something else.

She looked with terror, as her fingers became longer, double their original length. Her eyes turned to crystal white she tumbled to the floor, writhing in pain. Her breathing was faster now, her chest rising, and falling, she crunched herself into a ball. She could see her reflection in the glass of a shattered vial, her hair was turning grey, her skin became taught and wrinkly, stretched tight over the bones, and her screams were terrifying. Her horrible hands slashed at the air as her face changed. Her teeth became pointed; the jaws grew longer, like that of a werewolf. Blood spurted from her mouth, the monstrous teeth cutting through her lips. Animal like hair grew from her body. The once beautiful young woman was now a hideous creature of darkness.

Outside, the rain came down in a heavy downpour while thunder rattled the windows of the house, then a bolt of lightning struck a tree, sending sparks flying as a huge branch crashed to the ground. When the thunder roared this time, so did something else.

From deep within the mansion, horrible blood curdling screams rang through the darkness of the night. It wasn't human. It was more like a screaming wolf and banshee together.

Inside the mansion, the light flickered in the laboratory, casting a hideous shadow upon the wall. The shadow reared back its head, holding its twisted clawed hands to the heavens, screaming again. Pointed canine teeth, were daggers, cast upon the damp plaster. The creature walked over to the dead man's body, and knelt beside him. With one whip of its claws, split the stomach open and ate the flesh. Blood dripped from her hideous face. For half an hour, it ate, until the body was half devoured. She ran screaming from the house like a banshee from hell, into a nearby wooded area, and there she hid away from the real world only coming out at night to hunt.

*Twenty years later…*

A rich real estate tycoon, Harold Gibbons purchased the old mansion, and set to work turning it into a hotel that he would call "The Palace Hotel." He'd heard the stories surrounding the mansion, but dismissed them as absolute rubbish saying

"That every old house, particularly big old, spooky, mansions always have a ghost story or two attached to them."

Harold was a heavyset man in his forties. His balding head, handlebar moustache, mutton-chop sideburns, and expensive three-piece suits made him stand out in the crowd, along with his big booming arrogant voice. He liked to flash his cash, often taking huge rolls of hundred-dollar bills from his pocket, paying for people's drinks at his rich playboy clubs. He smoked Cuban cigars, drank expensive cognac, while boasting about his fortune, and how well his shares in real estate and oil were doing. He had no time for ordinary working people. To Harold, they were nothing more than a thorn in his side, always looking for more money or staging work stoppages.

He forgot that his father, Harold Gibbons Sr. was an ordinary worker, but well-liked by everyone. He used to work in a steel works factory, pouring the molten metal from the huge steel casks into the awaiting moulds to form a steel girder or whatever it was to become. It was at this factory that he was blinded in one eye by a red-hot metal spark that flew from one of the moulds one day. He wore an eye patch over his left eye for the rest of his days.

Now, Harold Jr. was a super-rich multi-millionaire, but disliked by many people. His newest venture, the old Bradford Mansion, was to be his crowning glory. He invested thousands into it. Making every room fit for a king and the staying price a king's ransom. For a year, the construction continued, until things started to happen. Dead, half-eaten animals turned up at the site.

The workers were nervous, even refusing to work there after dark because of the stories of the creature that haunted the place.

One morning, an enraged Harold Gibbons, came to the mansion, when his chauffeur driven car came to a stop he got out. His Bolar hat made his chubby, heavy, face look like a bulldog in clothes. He marched up to the supervisor of the construction company and slammed his horse head walking cane on the desk.

"What the hell is going on here? Am I not paying you enough already? Why are your workers refusing to work? Have you no authority here? I want this hotel finished, ready for its grand opening in four months' time, or do I have to hire someone better?" Gibbons barked at the young supervisor.

"Look, Mr. Gibbons, my workers will not work here after sundown. They know the story of old Bradford. There have been half eaten animals turning up on the site. And the men are afraid," Will Jones said, standing up from behind his desk.

"You pathetic idiots, you're working near a forest where wild animals live. The dead creatures that are turning up are more than likely left-over kills by wolves, foxes or whatever. Your superstitions are costing me dearly. I want you, and your men to work doubly hard to get this place finished, or so help me, you won't see another damn cent," Gibbons yelled grabbing his walking cane storming out of the office.

For the next few days, the men worked from dawn until dusk. One night, four of the men stayed on to finish off some electrical work. The sun went down fast, and night soon arrived. From the woods, something watched them. One man stayed outside working on a fuse box, whistling to himself. He was cutting a wire when something moved behind him and knocked over an aluminium bucket.

"Christ, what the hell?" he screamed slipping from his ladder with fright. He got to his feet, and looked around, but there was nothing.

"If that's you Mulligan, I'm gonna kick your Irish ass," The man shouted as he reached the overturned bucket.

There was nothing there, he turned around and a raccoon scurried out from behind a pile of timber planks and squealed as the man trod on it.

"Oh, Fuck!" he screamed, falling backwards, landing on his ass.

"Get out of here you little meatball," Throwing a stick at the creature. It ran to the woods and scurried up a tree. The man laughed, getting to his feet, dusting himself down. He bent over to pick up his hard hat, looking to his left; there before him were two hideous clubbed, clawed feet. He swallowed hard, and stood; His eyes opened wide with fear when the thing of legend whipped its claws, tearing his throat open in a flash. Tattered flesh dangled from his neck, and blood poured down his chest. He made a horrible gurgling sound sinking to his knees. The thing hissed at him, grabbing, him by the jacket collar, dragging him into the woods at great speed. A trailing pool of blood is all that remained.

The other workers came from the mansion a short time later.

"Joe, where are you?" They called out. They walked to where he was last working. They found his hard hat with the trail of blood, and fear struck every man. They gazed at the gruesome mess, shivers running up and down their spines, they backed away, their eyes scanning everywhere before fear made them run to their waiting car and speed away.

An hour later, the police arrived at the site along with the supervisor, after that Harold Gibbons came. It was now after eleven thirty, and Gibbons was not too happy being called away from his Tuesday night game of poker. He walked towards the Chief of police and the supervisor.

"What the hell is going on here?" He bellowed standing before them.

"There's been a murder here Harold. Joe Crockett was killed. We found his remains in the back woods," the supervisor Will Jones stopped the Chief of police.

"Remains, that's what you're calling it? He was torn apart." Will said with a wild stare, towering over the police officer

"Will, I know you're upset by Joe's death, but let me handle this okay?" Chief of police Eric Rogers said looking to Gibbons.

"Harold, until we know who or what killed Joe Crockett, I'm afraid we will have to shut down the site. It's an official crime scene, and it's now a murder investigation," Eric said looking at Gibbons ever-reddening face.

"You are slowing my development here Eric. A bear, wolf, or something, more than likely killed the man. You men are getting far too superstitious over this so-called beast of Bradford Mansion." Rogers cut Gibbons short.

"Harold, there are no bears or wolves in these parts. Something or someone is responsible for this brutal murder, and I intend to catch him," Eric walked away to talk to one of his deputies.

"Damn you Gibbons," Will Jones exclaimed with poison in his voice, spitting on the ground when he turned to walk away.

"You're fired Jones. Do you hear me? Fired," Gibbons yelled.

Jones turned, and punched Gibbons in the mouth, knocking him to the ground. A police deputy held him back. Gibbons looked up at them with blood dripping from his nose.

"I want this man arrested. I want to press charges for assault," Gibbons said, getting to his feet, taking a tissue from his pocket. The deputy released Will Jones.

"I hope you're happy with yourself Gibbons. How many more have to die before you listen. My company is pulling out of here first thing tomorrow morning. I hope that bitch kills you next," Will barked before he stormed off getting into his car.

In the backwoods, Eric Rogers walked around with his flash light, looking at the place where Joe Crockett's butchered body was found. He knelt to examine the area looking at the strange footprints in the soil.

"Damn! What if it is a bear? There's no creature I ever saw with feet like this," He was saying to himself, when something moved in the shadows, he shone his light to where the noise seemed to come from.

There was nothing. His left hand dropped to his side drawing his pistol. He moved the flash light to the right and back to the left.

The creature was watching him. His light briefly shone on her face, she hissed vanishing back into the woods. The cop fired four shots alerting the rest of his deputies. Six armed men came to his side. Eric stood there trembling, looking white as snow.

"What is it Chief?" A deputy asked, approaching Eric. He swallowed hard.

"I saw her. She's real," he said in a shaky voice.

"Saw what Chief? What's real?" the same deputy asked, gazing into the woods.

"The beast, she's real. She killed Crockett. All right spread out. If you see the bitch, shoot to kill," Rogers gave the orders and they entered the woods, their lights scanning everywhere.

The beast was watching them. She hid behind a tree when a light beam shone toward her. A cop put his hand in his pocket, pulling out his cigarettes. He put one in his mouth and was about to light up when the beast attacked. Her clawed hand punched through his back and appeared through his stomach. Blood flowed from his mouth pain making his body tremble like a hundred volts of electricity was running through him. It pulled its hand back, with a terrible, bubbling, sucking sound as she ripped his insides out from behind; she held the gruesome, bloody, mess in her disfigured hands.

The body fell to the ground, the creature walked into the blackness.

It wasn't too long before she found another cop, she came charging from the blackness slashing her claws at the cop's throat and like a ghost; she disappeared, while a decapitated body fell to the ground.

Eric Rogers was in front. He had seen the beast of legend and it frightened him so much that he was shooting at shadows. She was above him in the trees, and without warning, she dropped down on him screaming. The impact sent him flying face first into the ground, dropping his gun, he held his flash light in front of him, staring at the horrible thing gazing, and grimacing at him.

"Jesus, save me," he whimpered in fear, as she closed in on him. It picked him up and with its claws, tore his throat open. One by one, the other police officers met the same fate.

*Back at the mansion:*

Gibbons was inside looking at the plans and how much work still had to be done to his hotel. He was examining the blueprints when a door opened and closed with a bang startling him.

"Who's there? This is private property," he bellowed picking up his candle, the electricity should have been connected that evening, but that night's events prevented the electricians from finishing their work.

He walked into the corridor, the candle flickering, casting shadows on the walls. Every step he took the candle flickered. Just as he turned a corner, from the darkness the beast breathed heavy extinguishing the flame.

"Goddammit, where did I put those matches?" He snapped at himself fumbling around in his pockets.

He halted, with a look of fear on his face; eyes opened wide, breathing becoming faster. His hands trembled; he thought he felt something breathing on his neck. He found the matches and re-lit the candle with his hands still shaking. The light of the candle hardly lit the dark hallway.

He turned around to see what was there. Nothing, there was nothing. He breathed a sigh of relief.

"Damn fool, you're letting your mind play tricks with you," he thought to himself turning around to go back to the office.

He looked in front of him and screamed, there before him stood the beast. She was taller than Gibbons and she bared her horrible teeth. She grabbed him, and the candle tumbled from his hands to the floor and went out. His screams echoed throughout the mansion, then silence, apart from a terrible ripping, cracking, sound as she tore Gibbons apart, then she roared.

From that day on, the old Bradford house became known as Devils Mansion, a place even the bravest of men dared not venture.

After the slaughter on that terrible night, the Mansion was abandoned and forgotten. These days, it's used by teenagers for drinking, drugs, and wild parties. Tonight, one such wild party will take place, and the wildest party animal of them all, will make her presence known. The drink may flow, but its blood that will spill. The music will be loud, but so will their screams. This is her home, and they were not invited. Once being renovated to be a hotel; Devil's Mansion is one place you don't want to spend a night. Elizabeth waits to greet you with open jaws and claws from hell. At Devil's Mansion, you'll be checking in, but you won't be checking out alive!

Ben, Jackie, Roger, and Sarah sat at the mall enjoying a cool soda pop. They were talking about what happened when they met for their second date how they came across the Satanists and defeated the demon.

"Ha! Ha! Oh, how time flies. That was two years ago now, and man, have we gone up against real nastiness since then," Roger said with a laugh.

"Yeah, we sure have. It's hard to believe it happened two years ago, and that we're still together," Ben remarked reaching over holding Jackie's hand. She smiled at him.

"I hear there's a party going on tonight over at the old Bradford Mansion, might be fun," she winked placing her hand between Ben's legs. Sarah sat up in her seat.

"Devil's Mansion, are you going crazy girl? You know the stories as well as I do, about that damn place," she said in a loud tone.

"What's the story with the mansion?" Roger looked at her in puzzlement.

The girls told the story, and after they finished, they all took a rain check.

"If that's true, and there's a party going on, what if that creature shows up for some fun of her own?" Ben asked with a serious look on his face.

"Relax Ben. It's only a legend, and there have been parties at that old place for years and nothings ever happened," Jackie took a sip of her drink.

"I don't know baby. I didn't believe in aliens until one turned up on our doorstep and thought Leather Face only existed in the movies until Harry Gordon came to town. So, you can't be too careful, can you?" Ben turned to look at Roger.

*Back at the mansion:*

In the basement where the old man's laboratory used to be, two teens really got hot and heavy. Sabrina Byram was a real man-mad bitch, who has had more men than God knows what. She was tall, slim, and had long, straight, black hair, a huge bust, and a black rose tattoo on her left breast. Her skin-tight leather pants, put tears in the eyes of a good deal of young testosterone charged males. Mike McCormick was a fourteen-year-old virgin. His friends had set him up so he could lose his virginity to Sabrina. Mike was a shy, quiet, average guy who never had a girlfriend, not that he was ugly or anything. He didn't have the nerve to ask anyone out, so his friends went behind his back and set him up with Sabrina, and he was getting places with her.

They were lying on the floor on a makeshift bed getting heavier, and hotter, by the minute. He slipped his hand inside her pants when something moved in the shadows. Sabrina stopped kissing him sitting up listening.

"Why did you stop?" he asked, disappointed.

"Did you hear something?" she looked at him.

"I heard nothing," he said kissing her neck.

"Oh well, back to business," She took off her top, revealing her huge breasts again. Something moved, this time they both heard it.

"I told you there was something moving. See what it is," She demanded, holding her top in front of her to cover her exposed breasts.

Mike stood up, with a pissed off look on his face slipping on his T-shirt. He looked at Sabrina.

"Well, go on," she said sarcastically lighting up a cigarette.

"Jeez, all right, I'll go," he walked into the shadows and stopped, looking around with a look of concern on his face as he thought of the old legend. Something moved suddenly making him jump.

"Oh! Fuck," he whimpered, swallowing, walking toward the strange sounds.

When he got closer, he could see a shadow on the wall, and with caution moved toward it. Suddenly, three young men jumped out at him. He stifled a scream as he stumbled backward, landing on his ass. The guys just laughed.

"What, the hell are you doing here?" He asked keeping his voice low.

"Oh! Mike, we had to come and see if you would actually do it, we were setting up the generator and the rest of the gear for tonight and decided to check in on you," one of them said with a big smile.

In the shadows, the beast watched a hideous look on her monstrous face. She moved around to get a closer look. She saw the four of them laughing and talking. Then one guy felt he had something breathing on his neck, He screamed as a horrible hand came from the shadows, dragging him into the darkness.

The others stood there shivering when a cascade of blood flew from the shadows splattering them. Fear got a hold of them and they ran.

Sabrina heard the commotion.

"Mike, what's going on what have you done?" she looked at his blood-dappled face. She was backing away from them when the creature appeared behind her.

"Sabrina, behind you," they screamed. She turned around and looked death in the face; her mouth was open ready to scream when it hissed. Its claws slashed through the air, ripping her head from her body. The others ran fast as they could, but in their panic, didn't realize they were running the wrong way. The beast screamed.

"Oh! Shit, it's coming," one of the frightened trio exclaimed as they tried to hide in the darkest corner they could find. The beast came into full view and stopped. It looked around sniffing at the air. The three young men were so frightened that they didn't realize that it could hear their heart's pounding with her acute sense of hearing. Without warning, it rushed at them.

"Fuck, run," Mike yelled as they bolted for an open doorway.

The creature was on them in a flash. Two made it through the doorway, just when the last was running through the beast dragged him back screaming, the door slammed with a loud bang. The other two looked behind and saw blood flowing beneath the door. They ran again. The creature's cries echoed through the mansion as they got to the front door.

"We made it," Mike smiled while the other teen reached for the door handle.

The beast dropped from the stairway, and grabbed him by the hair, lifting him off the ground as he kicked and screamed. It tore his throat out; he shook and choked on his own blood. Mike peed his pants when the creature stared at him, dropping the body turning toward him. He backed away from her with fear on his face, pleading, with her not to kill him.

"Please, don't kill me," he begged, tears in his eyes, but it roared, taking his head off with one vicious swipe. Then there was a deathly silence. The killings had started again.

🕯

The four were walking around town when a girl in her early teens, approached them. Jackie used to babysit her when she was only five years old. Rebecca McCormick looked like something from a horror movie with her dental train track braces, you couldn't see her teeth only the metal. She was worried about her brother.

"I haven't seen him since ten this morning. He said he was going to the old Bradford Mansion," she was worried for his safety Jackie and the others were now.

"Hey, come on Rebecca I'm sure he's fine. He's been drinking with his friends, got drunk and passed out that's all. Never mind those old stories you heard. They're only ghost stories made up to keep teenagers away from the place," Jackie stopped and looked at Rebecca, her eyes watered and she looked at the ground. Ben felt sorry for her and placed his hand on her shoulder.

"Rebecca, if it makes you feel better, we can go look for your brother at that creepy old mansion. As Jackie said they've just had too much to drink and lost track of time," he said with a smile.

Rebecca smiled back at him.

"Will you? You know the stories about that place, I hope Mike is all right," She had sadness in her voice as she stared into the distance. Roger looked at Ben, saw that gleam in his eye, and he knew Ben was just looking for a little excitement. All four of them walked back to Jackie's to collect the car and their flash lights.

"Hey, come on, hopefully it's nothing. We'll check it out anyway. You never know what we could find," Ben smiled a huge grin, starting the engine of the Mustang, tearing down the road in a cloud of dust.

Twenty minutes later, they arrived at the mansion. They got out of the car and looked up at the huge building. Ben whistled.

"This place must be worth a fortune, look at the size of it," he exclaimed lighting up a smoke when he walked up the six steps to the front door. The door was ajar as they neared it, Blackness creeping through the crack, they switched on their torches as Roger eased the door open with an eerie squeak that echoed through the main lobby.

From the ceiling hung a massive dust ridden chandelier with cobwebs and spiders to match. They had the place decorated in a rich wine colour now faded with age. Decades had worn the carpeting that was once dark red into nothing more than a mouldy looking old rug.

Decades of dust covered the reception desk in thick layers hiding the dark mahogany worktop.

"All right, that's enough sight-seeing. Let's find the kid and get out of here," Ben said glancing at the others.

When he walked toward them, something caught his eye behind the front door gleaming in the torch-light. He looked over Jackie's shoulder and Sarah looked at him.

"Ben, what are you doing?" she watched as he closed the door to have a look at what was on the ground. He knelt on one knee.

"Come over here now," he said in a loud tone and they surrounded him.

"What have you found?" Roger asked, fixing his glasses.

Ben reached out his hand and with his finger, ran it through the liquid on the floor. He rubbed his fingers together and brought it closer to his face then stood.

"It looks like blood, let's find the kid, and get the hell out of here. I'm wondering about those stories. If it is blood, where did it come from and who was bleeding?" he asked with a serious look on his face now.

"Mike, where are you?" Sarah bellowed her voice echoing through the mansion. From the shadows, it watched them, her claws scratching the timber of a doorway.

"Did you hear something?" Roger asked, looking behind him.

"Easy, Roger don't let this place play tricks with your mind," Ben said looking back at him.

Jackie yelled from the hallway.

"What did you find?" Sarah asked coming up beside her. She giggled holding up a pair of panties. They laughed.

"Oh, now we know why he's late getting back. Oh, the joys of puberty," Ben said with a big grin.

He wasn't smiling for too long, for just a few steps up the hall they came across another pool of blood. Roger swallowed hard, and they looked at each other. Something moved behind them.

"I think the legend of Bradford Mansion is more than a legend. It's here," Ben whispered.

The creature screamed, sending chills through them. They turned around to look behind them and there stood the beast. She was horrible; her twisted clawed hands, long jaws and pointed teeth, grey animal hair all over her body; words could not describe the monstrosity that now stood before them.

"Stay together and run," Ben grabbed Jackie's hand and they took off running toward the old laboratory.

It screamed again, chasing after them. Roger and Sarah were right beside them as they got to the room that used to be the old man's lab. They slammed the door and pushed a heavy desk against it while the beast roared, hammering at the door. They backed away from it watching the barricade shudder with every strike. Jackie screamed when she looked at the floor. There was the headless corpse of Sabrina Byram, the butchered remains of Mike McCormick and his friend's and then from elsewhere in the mansion a generator started up and soon after loud music boomed, shaking the house. The beast roared, her hoofed clawed feet thudding the floor as she ran through the hallway towards the music.

"Fuck the party has started she's going to kill them. What are we going to do?" Sarah asked looking at Ben. Jackie began removing the barricade, and the others joined her.

The party was in full swing, where teenagers were drinking, smoking marijuana, getting hot and heavy with the girls. The music blared, and strobe lights flashed, as the beast entered the room. Her claws sliced through the air, the strobe lighting making them look like silver blades. Blood splashed on a girl on the floor when the guy dancing beside her had his face slashed to ribbons. She screamed, as the thing looked at her with rage in its eyes. A panic broke out, and terror-stricken teenagers tried to run through the narrow doorway to escape the slaughter behind them. The screaming continued, ten people were dead, the rest trampling each other trying to get away. Four figures came charging up the hallway through the stampede of frightened teens. People ran screaming for their lives. When they reached the doorway, the beast was there with open arms to greet them with the angry look on her horrible face, nothing remained in the room where the party was, only a bloody mess, but she was only getting started.

"Oh, shit! She looks pissed off," Roger said, looking at the thing grimacing back at them.

"We have to destroy her once and for all. We can take her," Jackie said, looking at Ben with a smile.

He smiled back "I couldn't have said it better myself," he winked.

They stood together as it moved toward them, her eyes snow-white with rage. Without warning, she rushed at them screaming, slashing, her claws. They split to either side of her as she whizzed by, she stopped then turned around for another charge. "You're going down you ugly-looking bitch," Jackie yelled, grabbing a heavy candlestick from a desk.

It rushed at them again; Ben stepped to the left sticking out his leg sending it stumbling toward Jackie. She swung the candlestick striking the beast in the head. It roared in agony, blood soaking through her matted white hair over her hideous face.

Jackie stood there with a smile,

"How do you like that bitch?" she grinned; the beast swung its claws missing her by mere inches.

Ben punched it in the mouth twice pushing it back to Roger, who kicked out pushing it to Sarah. It went wild, screaming, and hollering, swinging its claws everywhere. Sarah looked on the ground and saw a broken mop handle with a nasty looking point, she picked it up and drove it through the creature's stomach. It stood there, ripping it from her gut, throwing it to the ground. Ben ran up kicking her again, sending her flying backward against the wall. There was a rusted steel spike protruding from the plaster. The creature screamed a horrible scream when the steel rod pierced through her chest. She screamed, holding on to the spike, trying to wrench it from her body, but it was too late. It had pierced through her heart and blood dribbled from her twisted mouth, she clawed at Ben. Jackie screamed, pounding its head again and again with the candlestick. Blood spewed everywhere until it moaned and stopped moving. Its head fell to its chest and it let out its last breath. The four looked at each other when it shrivelled up and decayed, turning to ash in an instant.

A bright light appeared behind them. As they turned around, the spirit of a beautiful young woman appeared smiling.

"Thank you," she said, disappearing with a smile.

Elizabeth was free of her terrible curse, and the beast of Devil's Mansion was no more.

"I think it's time to go home," Ben said, putting his arm around

Jackie's waist. In the distance police sirens blared coming closer and closer.

"Let the survivors tell the cops what happened. We've done our part," he said with a grin.

"Another demon sent back to hell. Man, are we good? Or are we good?" Roger said with a smile still on a high after the fight. The others just laughed as they walked on down the road to the car and drove off into the distance.

Six months later they tore the old Bradford mansion down and all that remained was a pile of rubble, but deep under its foundations, a maze of tunnels lay undiscovered. A shadow appeared upon the walls, its vicious clawed hands, pointed canine teeth, and long matted hair. It reared its head back, hissing in a mocking evil grimace, she was laughing. Elizabeth's soul was free, but the beast lives on, her tortured, horrible body damned to live forever in the darkness of the caves, never again to see the light of day. Such is the price of immortality.

# HARRY GORDON'S BLOODY REVENGE

✠

There was a buzz of excitement in the air at Ben and Jackie's early one morning. Ben was in the kitchen making breakfast when Jackie walked in with a big smile on her face. She was trying hard to contain her excitement, but couldn't hold back any longer. She ran up to Ben, agitation running through her like electricity, flinging her arms around her man and kissing him.

"What's all this?" he asked with a little laugh.

"Ben, I've just done a pregnancy test, and it's positive. I'm pregnant," she said with a smile.

"This is great. I will be a dad," he lifted her up in his arms, gazing into her deep blue eyes, kissing her.

*But their happiness will be cut short…*

On the outskirts of town, in the desert wasteland, deep inside a cave, a hulking figure sat by a fire.

"It's time to make you pay, bitch! You'll be begging for death long before you are dead, and your little friends won't be able to save you this time. You're all going to die!" Harry screamed, standing up, revving the saw raising it high above his head.

He left the cave soon after the sun had gone down, marching through the wasteland, his heavy footsteps leaving huge prints in the sand. On he marched, with rage in his eyes, the saw gripped so tight he could have snapped it in half. He came to a small wooded area, thoughts of the last time he came here shot through his memory, his teeth clenched with rage, he screamed, charging into the cover of the woods. He stopped after a few minutes right behind Jackie's house, staying in the shadows, watching.

Jackie pulled the curtains in the kitchen, Harry wanted to burst in, there and then, but he waited. A light flicked on upstairs; he could see Jackie undressing through the bathroom window. She was running water in the shower. He stepped out of the shadows to the small wooden gate, standing there, staring up at the window. Jackie reached to close the blind, and just happened to glance down. Harry raised the chainsaw above his head, grinning at her.

She screamed, recognizing him right away. Ben was up the stairs in a flash. He rushed into the bathroom, making Jackie jump with a little start. She covered herself with a towel.

"Are you okay?" he asked coming up beside her.

She was in tears, throwing her arms around him. He could feel her shivering.

"Jackie, what happened? What frightened you?" He tried to calm her.

"Harry Gordon! Harry Gordon was standing out there looking at me," she sobbed.

Ben looked shocked with what she said.

"Harry Gordon's long-gone baby! You sliced him up good. I know the police didn't find his body and two policemen died, but he knows better than to mess with you now," he said with a smile, trying to make her feel better.

She looked at him with anger in her eyes.

"He was out there Ben. He was, what if he's come back to get us after what we did to him? Do you remember the demons? You know what that saw can do. Do you want him to hurt us again? Do you want those demons to come back?" Her deep blue eyes had a sincerity he couldn't deny.

"Stay here and lock the door. He could be in the house," He bolted out of the bathroom.

"Ben, Don't ---," that's all she could say as she slammed the door and locked it. Ben's footsteps echoed throughout the house as he ran down the stairs; she backed away from the door as if it was a monster.

Ben had been cleaning out the attic a few days before and found her father's old shotgun along with some shells. The gun was in perfect order, apart from a decade of dust on the barrel. Down in the kitchen, he loaded the gun snapping it shut.

"Right, you son of a bitch. You better run if you don't want your ass full of lead," he said to himself flicking on the outside light. He slowly opened the back door stepping out with the gun to his shoulder. He aimed into the darkness, his eyes scanning everywhere.

Slowly he walked toward the back gate and stopped, bent down on one knee, and sure enough, there were two huge footprints in the soft earth.

"Son of a bitch, you were here," he was saying to himself when a noise made him stand up and take aim.

Something moved in the shadows, he fired a shot into the air. The figure came closer. He pushed the butt of the gun hard into his shoulder and waited. Closer and closer it came. His finger curled around the second trigger as the figure got to the gate it stopped. A heavy breath came from the silhouette when it came into the gentle glow of the outside light.

"You scared the shit out of me," a voice said. Ben breathed a sigh of relief, lowering the gun.

"I scared you. I could have blown you away," he said looking at Roger who had turned pale.

Ben activated the safety catch on the gun placing it over his shoulder, they both walked back to the house.

"What the hell were you doing out there with that gun?" Roger asked getting over the shock.

"Harry fucking Gordon's back, that's what I was doing out there," Ben replied as he removed the spent shell and good one from the gun closing it up with a little snap, before placing it back in its cradle above the fireplace.

Upstairs Jackie was getting dressed when below she heard Ben and Roger.

"Harry Gordon's long gone," Roger said as he sat down looking at Ben with a confused look. Jackie appeared in the doorway.

"He was out there Rodge, looking at me upstairs," she sat beside him.

"That's why I fired when I saw you coming at me. I thought you were him. Goddammit, you know what happened the last time he showed up. That damn chainsaw of his did something to the people he killed and the one's he'd only injured also turned nasty. Jackie sliced him up good, but he still lives. That saw is the key, I am certain of that now. Jackie thinks he's come back for his revenge, and she could be right," Ben stopped for a while folding his arms in deep concentration before continuing...

"Come to think of it, Jackie left that damn machine beside the body after she mangled him. The next thing you know he's restored back to his full psychotic self. We must destroy that blade, and once it's gone, maybe he can die, because as long as he still has it in his possession, we don't have a snowball's chance in hell of killing the bastard. And how come you were out in the woods Roger? He could have killed you!" Ben lit up a smoke.

"I was taking a shortcut. Now, if Gordon has come back for his revenge. What's stopping him coming back when you're asleep?" Roger asked.

"He's got a point Jackie. We can't stay here while he's around, it's too dangerous," He walked to the sitting room window. A serious expression crossed his face as he stared into the blackness.

"You will stay with me and Sarah until we get him," Roger said, standing up, zipping up his black leather jacket.

"Jackie, put on your jacket. We're out of here," Ben said, putting on his own jacket. He locked the door and they walked up the dreary road. They were not alone, from the darkness of the woods, Harry followed.

They walked the half mile to Sarah's house without a word, looking all around them like scared school kids, watching out for the boogeyman. Roger placed the key in the door and they went inside. Harry watched from the shadows as the door closed.

Sarah was lying on the sofa when they walked in.

"Hey. What brings you here this late?" She said, standing up hugging them both. Jackie sat down and told her the story.

"I don't believe it. That creep was standing outside watching you undress?" Sarah was yelling, gritting her teeth so hard she could have broken a tooth. Jackie nodded her head with tears in her eyes. Sarah hugged her as she cried.

"If he's back, and he's already killed someone. You know what that chainsaw does to the people it cuts or kills," Sarah was yelling again.

"Calm down Sarah. We've already thought of all that. What he did to Will and the others," Ben shook off his jacket, slung it over a chair and continued talking.

"I don't think he's killed anyone yet. I think he's just after us, after what we did to him. We're all together now so we have a fighting chance," as he was speaking Jackie stood.

"I'll make us some coffee," she said, leaving the room for the kitchen. As she filled the kettle, she felt a draft. The back door was open, and she shivered with fear walking towards it. Her shaking hand reached out and closed it. She turned the key with a click and let out a sigh of relief. When she turned to go back, a feeling of dread crept over her that made her mouth go dry, just in time, something caught her attention, and she glanced to her right. A look of horror appeared on her face; her heart pounded with fear as Harry towered over her with an evil grin on his face.

"Hello Killer. It's payback time," he growled, his huge hand grabbing her by the throat lifting her off the ground.

She gagged for breath; her eyes half closed. She lost consciousness momentarily but tried to kick out at him as she choked. Harry's eyes were alive with rage, his huge hand gripping tighter and tighter, then he threw her against the wall. She slammed off it with a bang and lay on the floor face down. Harry locked the side door that led from the hallway to the kitchen.

He kicked Jackie three times in the ribs; she coughed and gagged before he turned her over on her back with his foot. The door handle rattled and Harry laughed.

"Oh! How nice, your little buddies are coming to save you, too bad, they're too fucking late this time bitch, tonight you'll sleep in Hell," Harry screamed, as did the chainsaw.

Her mouth opened wide to scream, but no sound came out. Tears filled her eyes, agony running through her body when she felt the blade slice into her. The last thing she saw was Gordon's horrible face grinning down on her before passing out. Gordon laughed, opened the back door, and took off running into the darkness, taking one last look at Jackie bleeding on the floor before he wandered off into the night.

Ben roared. "JACKIE," while he kicked in the door with all he had. The door shuddered, and with another kick gave way. They stood there in shock; Jackie lay in a pool of blood. She had been split open from hip to hip. Ben ran to her side with tears pouring down his face.

"Oh God, no!" he cried as he knelt and cradled her in his arms. Sarah ran to the sitting room, grabbing the phone to call for help.

Jackie was alive. Blood poured from her wound; Roger took off his sweater and folded it up placing it on the cut and applying pressure trying to bring the bleeding under control. Ben held her, kissing her forehead.

"Come on Jackie, don't die on me. Don't leave this way. This is not your time to go, not when you've got so much to live for. Come on baby stay with me," he whispered into her ear as he cried.

Her breathing was shallow now, and she turned pale and cold. He held her hand, her engagement ring sparkled, and he remembered the night he gave it to her. The same night Harry Gordon turned up. As he held her hand, she squeezed his.

She opened her eyes and looked at him.

"I'll always love you Ben," she whispered with a little smile before her head dropped to the left and lay on his chest.

He reared his head to the heavens and yelled. Sirens screamed in the distance as the paramedics raced to the scene, but they were too late. She had stopped breathing. Two paramedics rushed in, commencing C.P.R on Jackie. One of them inserted an intravenous line into her arm. For two minutes, they worked on her, but there was no response. Ben was crying his eyes out as was Sarah.

Roger stood there, too shocked to do anything. A paramedic yelled, "We have a pulse. I don't know how but she's breathing," he said as the other one wheeled in a stretcher.

They placed Jackie on a backboard and then placed her on the stretcher. They strapped her in and wheeled her out to the waiting ambulance. "She needs a blood transfusion ASAP or we will lose her," the paramedic said and closed the ambulance doors. Ben caught the door, ripping it from the paramedic's grasp. "I'm going with her," he growled climbing in.

🕯

The ambulance sped down the road, siren blaring into the night. Jackie was a fighter, and she was holding on with everything she had left. The fifteen-minute drive to the hospital seemed like an eternity, until the ambulance screeched to a stop outside the A&E Department of Cedar Sinai Medical Centre. The paramedics off loaded the stretcher and rushed through the doors where a medical team was standing by. An orderly took Ben to the waiting room where he sat down and cried. Fifteen minutes later, Roger and Sarah came in.

"How is she?" Roger asked, handing Ben a coffee.

"I don't know. They haven't told me anything yet," he sat there his gaze fixed on the coffee. Sarah sat beside him and hugged him.

🕯

For the next six hours, they stayed there. Sarah fell asleep across the couch. Roger was asleep in the armchair. Ben stood by the window; eyes bloodshot threatening to close at any moment. He needed sleep or pass out standing there. He turned to sit down, but paused when a doctor walked in. He woke the others.

The doctor sat down with them, his eyes watery from both tiredness and sadness.

"Ms. Anderson has had a narrow escape. If that cut had only been a few millimetres deeper, she wouldn't have survived long enough to reach the hospital. She has spent the past six hours undergoing emergency surgery. We have had to remove part of her small intestine, one of her ovaries; we also had to rebuild her uterus. She needed five pints of blood during the surgery. I have more grim news," the old surgeon stopped, looked at Ben and the others sitting there almost in a group hug arms around each other.

"Ms Anderson was pregnant and the child did not survive. By the looks of things, she was about four weeks into the pregnancy. I am sorry to have to tell you such, terrible news, it is never easy for neither doctor, nor loved ones, I am certain she will make a full recovery in time. I'm sorry," the old man said, shaking Ben's hand as he stood up

90

to leave.

"Can we see her?" Ben asked.

"Tomorrow, she is still sleeping under the anaesthetic," The doctor left the room.

Back at Sarah's place:

Harry was waiting. He already got Jackie. He wasn't going away until he finished them all. Jackie's blood still stained his saw, he held up the blade in front of his twisted face, he sniffed at the blood and licked it.

"So sweet, but revenge is even sweeter," he whispered then laughed. From the sitting room, he could see headlights coming up the driveway, it was the police. He stood and hid in the shadows, ready to strike.

Two cops entered the house, walking toward the kitchen where the attack took place.

"What kind of twisted mind has this bastard got? I mean no one deserves to be tortured like this," One cop said, looking down at the dried blood on the floor.

"I don't know what sort of deranged madman we're dealing with, but we'll get him soon enough. You know it could be the same guy that attacked these folks a few months ago. The story is the same, a huge guy wielding a chainsaw. God, it gives me the creeps thinking about it," the other cop said looking out the back door.

Harry crept from the shadows to the kitchen door. He could see the two cops talking with their backs to him. His eyes opened wide with rage; he came up behind the two men. The saw screamed into action.

"Surprise," He yelled as the blade flashed and a head rolled across the floor. The other cop drew his gun firing six shots at this raving lunatic.

"Ooh, that tickles," Harry, said, laughing at the cop who let his gun drop from his grasp as terror caught hold. Harry grabbed him by the throat with his huge hand lifting the terrified man off the ground. The man kicked and struggled to get free, but Harry only laughed revving the saw. The cop screamed when both his legs fell to the floor with a cascade of blood. Harry dropped the man who crawled on his belly trailing blood behind him. He dawdled behind the cop with slow steps enjoying seeing the legless man crawling along like a human snail. Harry grinned, and then the saw roared. Blood poured from the cop's mouth as the saw cut through his back, towards his skull, the engine came to a quiet stop. Harry stepped over the body, walking out the back door into the night.

In the hospital's car park, Ben, Roger, and Sarah were leaving the premises. Roger had driven Ben's Mustang to the hospital. They were all in the car with Roger at the wheel. They drove for about five minutes before Ben barked, "Pull the car over now."

Roger stopped the car.

"Are you all right Ben?" Sarah asked, watching him get out.

He stood there with his fists clenched, rage across his face. The other two got out and stood beside him. He looked at them both with a vicious look, his eyes were wide, pupils dilated, his teeth were grinding, and his breathing was heavy.

"We're going after Harry Gordon!" he said with poison in his voice.

"Ben, I know you are hurting but going after him is suicide. You know how strong he is. Do you think we can defeat him?" Roger asked with a slight look of fear in his eyes.

"You never know until you try. I owe it to Jackie to at least try, so do both of you. We can run and hide, but he'll find us. I'm sick of running, of being afraid, but not any more. I've never been as afraid as I was tonight when Jackie nearly lost her life because of that bastard. Harry Gordon must die, that damn chainsaw of his must be destroyed and him along with it. We're a team and I believe we were chosen for a reason. Was it destiny we all met? Was it fate that brought us all together? Look at the things we have faced already, huh! Is it a coincidence, it's us and us alone taking on the forces of darkness? Are we going to let evil win this day or are we going to rise to the challenge and kick evil's mother fucking ass right back to Hell? The buck stops here, we can defeat him. We have defeated other things that have come. We can do it, together. Are we going to live in fear? Are we going to let evil take over our lives? Or, are you going to join with me to become evils worst nightmare? We're the good guys here, it's down to us to keep evil at bay, and Harry Gordon deserves to burn in Hell, and before tonight is over, to hell he will go," He screamed raising his fists to the heavens, reared his head back, and gazed at the stars.

"We're with you all the way Ben. Let's kick his ass," Sarah yelled climbing back into the car.

Ben and Roger looked at each other.

"Do you think fate threw us together to fight the forces of darkness?" Roger asked raising an eyebrow.

"Oh, yeah" Ben said, getting angry again. Roger looked at the ground and then up at Ben.

"Okay, I'm with you. You drive," he said, running to the passenger door.

"You're going down Gordon." Ben said to himself when he got in and turned the key. Steam rose from the tires as the Mustang sped off into the night.

Ben was driving like a maniac running red lights, taking corners so fast the tires screeched.

"Where do we look?" Sarah asked, sitting between the two of them.

"Back at your place I've got a feeling he'll be waiting for us there," Ben replied gunning the engine speeding towards Sarah's house.

The Mustang screeched to a halt; Ben was out the door like a flash. A Police car had parked just a few feet in front of them and the front door was ajar. They looked at each other before they went inside, fear showed itself on each of their faces, but they knew what they had to do. The front door opened, they entered with extreme caution and stopped.

"Hello. Is anyone there?" Sarah yelled.

There was no reply. Roger tapped Ben on the shoulder. He turned around with Roger pointing to the floor, at the trail of blood that led to the kitchen.

"Fuck! He's already been here," Ben followed the blood trail to the kitchen. A decapitated body lay on the floor with the head lying there staring up at them, its eyes and mouth open with terror. Just beside them by the door, lay two severed legs.

Sarah gasped with fright following the trail of blood to the sitting room. "Oh my God," she exclaimed placing her hand over her mouth. The legless butchered body of the second cop lay behind the sofa. Ben walked over to it knelt on one knee reached out his fingers and touched the body.

"Ben, what are you doing?" Sarah asked in horror.

"It's still warm. He hasn't gone far," he said getting to his feet running to the back door flicking on the outside light. The others followed him.

He stood in the garden staring into the woods with a crow bar held in his hands. Roger had been busy tearing down an old timber shack during the week and left the bar beside the back door step.

"Where are you? You bastard, you want us? Then come and get us. Come on Gordon! Here we are," Ben screamed at the top of his voice. His fists clenched tight around the bar breathing heavy. Roger and Sarah looked around them. The tension was unbearable. Ben didn't move. He stood there staring.

"Come out and fight you son of a bitch. Come on, I'm waiting for you Gordon." he yelled again.

From the shadows, Harry laughed. "Ha-Ha-Ha-And I'm waiting for you too," he barked starting up the machine of death walking from the woods.

Ben's rage was off the scale.

"We're not afraid of you any more, Gordon. You killed my unborn child, nearly killed the woman I love, and now I will kill you," he pointed his finger at Harry.

"You talk too much. Shut the fuck up and let's dance,"

Harry growled, running at Ben. Roger and Sarah held their ground.

Harry's eyes opened wide with confusion when he saw Ben running at him. They both collided, sparks illuminated the night, the saw blade bouncing from the crowbar when Ben held it cross ways with both hands to deflect the saw attack. Harry backed off and kept the saw running holding it with one hand beckoning Ben to come and get it with a grin.

Ben punched Harry in the stomach and he swung the saw at Ben's head, he held up the bar but this time the bar went flying from his grasp and Gordon lost his balance for a second, Ben ran behind him. Harry turned around swinging the saw in a blinding arc; Ben saw it coming and ducked again. The saw shot over his head. Before Harry had time to recover, Ben punched him in the face again and again and again. Harry stumbled backwards. Ben's rage surprised him, but his rage was far more superior. Gordon screamed his huge hand clenched into a sledgehammer fist that slammed into Ben sending him flying back to Roger and Sarah. He lay on the ground looking up at them. The saw roared when Harry went on the attack. Roger helped Ben to his feet. Ben wanted to go at Harry again, but Roger held him back.

"Let me go, Roger I'll kill the bastard," he growled as Roger held him.

Harry came running at them chainsaw held to his chest.

"We must get that fucking saw away from him. It's his only weakness. Without it, he's fucked," Ben spat blood from his mouth.

They ran back through the house out the front door. The radio in the police car was broadcasting. Ben jumped in taking hold of the receiver and delivered a quick message before sparks flew from the car when Harry cut through the driver's door.

"Fuck!" Ben yelled, getting out the passenger side.

Sarah had the Mustang running when Ben jumped in, she spun the wheels and tore down the driveway. Harry stood there chainsaw above his head.

"Stop the car," Ben barked.

"Why?" asked Sarah.

"Just do it," Ben ordered. The car stopped, and he ran around to the driver's side. Sarah had slid over to the passenger side. Ben slammed the car into gear performing a U-turn and headed back to the house. He wasn't slowing. Harry was still in the driveway when the Mustang came hurtling at him from nowhere. His eyes opened wide when he was knocked off his feet as the car slammed into him, sending him flying over the roof. Ben jammed on the brakes turning his head, he looked over his shoulder.

"He still has a hold of that damn saw," He barked jamming the car into reverse. Harry sat upright, looking in horror when the car came at him again. There was a big bang; the car's occupants bumped up and down, as Gordon became a speed bump. The saw flew from his grasp.

"Now," Ben yelled as he leapt from the car.

Roger and Sarah grabbed the saw and ran down the road. In the distance, sirens wailed and red and blue lights flashed. Ben kicked Harry as he lay on the ground. Just as he was kicking him again Harry grabbed his leg, knocking him over.

"You can't kill me boy. Don't you know? I'm the devil's own," He growled, getting to his feet.

Ben rose to his feet and stood staring at Harry with rage in his eyes. Harry smiled a horrible smile as he ran at Ben.

Ben charged at him and they went punch for punch. Harry's fists were three times bigger than Ben's and with one mighty blow, sent Ben skating across the driveway. He lay there gasping for breath, blood pouring from his broken nose. Harry walked towards him laughing.

"Now you die," He barked picking Ben up from the ground.

His hands clamped around Ben's throat and he laughed all the while. Ben's eyes turned backward into his head the visions of Jackie dying in his arms went through his mind. He took one huge breath; his eyes popped open and with his right hand rammed his fingers into Harry's eyes. Harry dropped him, staggering around screaming, placing his hands over his injured eye. Ben kicked him in the stomach, and Harry bent over from the impact. Ben knocked him to the ground kneeling beside him punching with all he had.

"You got it wrong, you son of a bitch." he yelled, punching Harry several times.

"Now you die," he screamed, standing up and kicking Harry in the head.

Five police cars screeched to a halt in the driveway. Ben's rage kept him pounding at Harry. "Freeze," a police officer screamed his pistol aimed at Ben. He looked at the police officers with a blood-covered face, skinned elbows, and knuckles. Gordon was laughing on the ground. "Ha-Ha-Ha-Ha- You should have killed me when you had the chance," he said blood covering his teeth as he grinned.

It took six cops to restrain him and handcuff him to be taken away. Sarah and Roger came out of the shadows. "BEN," Sarah yelled, trying to get past the police and newspaper reporters. They still had the saw.

"Give it here now!" Ben barked, taking the saw from Sarah.

"That's incriminating evidence," a cop said, trying to take the saw from him. Ben and Roger ran to the back of the house to the garden shed where Roger kept his tools and appeared with a sledgehammer.

"Finish it," he yelled handing it to Ben.

Two cops came around the corner

"Drop the hammer now," one of them yelled.

"Fuck you," Ben snapped, raising the sledgehammer above his head yelling as he brought it down with a bang. It did nothing to the blade. He hit the saw two more times, but didn't even scratch it. They all looked at each other in amazement. Without warning, a dark figure appeared from a cloud of smoke.

"I believe this belongs to me," The man said, bending over to pick up the chainsaw.

Ben gripped the hammer, as the man in black stood up, the chainsaw gleaming in the moonlight. The cops drew their guns.

"Drop the saw now," one of them ordered. The man only laughed and walked away. The cops opened fire, and he stood there laughing. He looked at Ben and Roger, his eyes glowing red.

"I'll be back, I won't stop until the four of you are dead," He snapped.

"We'll be waiting, you god forsaken son of a bitch," Ben growled, the man laughed, vanishing before their eyes.

The two cops couldn't believe what they had just seen.

"How are you going to put that in a report?" Ben asked with a grin.

The cops looked at each other "Report what. We didn't see a damn thing," they said as they all walked around to the front

"What will happen to Harry Gordon?" Sarah asked.

"He'll be placed in a high security institution for the criminally insane. I don't think you'll have to worry about him for a long time. Now if, you'll excuse me, we have a lot of work to get done," the cop said going inside the house.

Four weeks later Jackie came home against doctor's orders. But she was missing Ben, Roger, and Sarah so much she had to get out. Harry Gordon was gone but another two victims met a grisly end, and a life not even begun ended inside of Jackie on that night of terror that was now over, or was it?

Six weeks later, during a vicious storm, the power dropped, lights flickered on and off. Machinery hummed to a silent stop, the lightning strike shutting off the electric fences surrounding the mental asylum. Lightning flashes and thunder rolls characterized the sky. A door creaked open, and the body of a security guard hit's the ground. A huge figure dashed for the fence, the rain soaking his clothes, wind blowing strong, a faint flash of lightning lit up the darkness, illuminating the figure that was already climbing the fence. When he landed on the ground outside, he looked back at the building and laughed.

"You can't stop me. No one can," he screamed and ran off into the night. A blinding flash of lightning struck the fence, sending sparks flying; once again Harry Gordon was out for vengeance.

# DAMON RAVENBLOOD

# DIMENSIONS OF TERROR

I t was a night like any other, and our four heroes were together at the Aces High nightclub, where they all met four years earlier. They were standing at the bar, drinking their beer, and talking.

"I can't believe it's four years ago, Roger and I bumped into both of you and spilled your drinks, but you apologized to us regardless," Ben took a sip of his drink.

Jackie laughed. "I know you owed us the apology, but you looked so cute that night I knew I wanted you. Ha-ha and I got you too, didn't I?" She kissed him.

"You got me hook, line, and sinker baby. Here's a toast to eternity, because my love I'm never letting you go, you're stuck with me now," Ben said with a smile.

"I know I am stuck with you, God help me," she replied with a wink and a smile, letting him know what was on her mind. She glanced over at Roger and Sarah, who were kissing and Ben leaned in to do the same.

Outside, rain belted out of the heavens, lightning flashed, and thunder rolled. They had enough of memory lane and decided it was time they left the nightclub. Just as they were walking out, this fool tried it on with Jackie. He came over and hugged her, trying grab her huge breasts. "Get off me, you creep," she yelled as the guy tried to kiss her.

Ben came charging from nowhere in a fit of jealous rage, grabbing the guy by the hair and pulling him back. The man looked at Ben and pulled a knife. Ben grimaced as the knife flashed past his face. He punched the guy in the face, knocking him to the ground. The bouncers saw what had happened and intervened, stepping between Ben and the assailant who lay on the floor, blood flowing from his nose and split lip. The doormen dragged him to his feet leading him away while he protested his innocence, "I did nothing. It was that guy who started it,"

The others had walked away and were on their way home.

"Fucking creep," Jackie screamed while Ben still looked mad as hell.

"Nobody will ever put a hand on you again. Not while, I'm around," he growled. Jackie smiled, holding his hand.

Just as they were walking past the power generator, a massive bolt of lightning struck it, sending sparks flying.

"Holy shit," Ben yelled, putting his arm over his head.

Without warning, the generator went into convulsions as it spun at twenty times its normal rate. A howling wind blew, and a bright light appeared to form a vortex, like a tornado of fire. The gaping hole whirled around, its energy reaching out and dragging them into the void.

"Fucking hell we're being pulled in," Sarah screamed.

"Everybody grab on to each other and don't let go no matter what happens," Ben yelled as he felt his feet leaving solid ground. They dangled in mid-air, levitated by the force of the vortex, suddenly they shot across the street at lightning speed as it pulled them in spinning them around and down, flames and demons raced past them as they fell. They screamed as they fell ten feet as the whirling fire wind spat them out, and they landed with a heavy thump in a huge sand pit.

⚰

They lay there motionless; an unreal heat beat down on them from the glow of two suns. Ben moaned and moved. The others woke up as well.

"Is everyone all right?" He asked, straightening his legs out in front of him. They nodded their heads and sat looking at each other before getting to their feet. A thirty-foot jagged rock face towered over them.

"Ah shit! If we want to get out of here, we have to climb out," Roger kicked at the sand. Something moved beneath the sand behind Ben, who was still staring at the rock face unaware of what was under him.

"Oh well, let's get moving," he took a step forward.

Something sprung up from the sand, grabbed his ankle, pulling him off his feet.

"Fucking hell," he yelled, looking down at his leg.

A giant tentacle wrapped around his ankle, dragging him backward. "BEN," Roger yelled as he and the girls grabbed a hold of his arms.

"Pull for god's sake before he disappears altogether," Sarah said as they pulled with all their might to free Ben, who was now up to his waist in the sand.

They pulled and slowly he emerged. As they heaved at Ben, something else came up with him. It was some kind of giant sand squid and it still had a hold of him, its razor-sharp beak open, ready for the kill. It looked like the squid from twenty thousand leagues under the sea, but this thing was a mutant and it was hungry. Jackie screamed, Ben looked back under his arm, and then stared back at the others.

"Pull harder," he yelled as another tentacle lashed through the air.

He used his free leg to kick at the tentacle that held him. Again, and again he kicked, but it still held fast. Another tentacle was whipping through the air when just in time they pulled Ben free, the thing roared, retracting its tentacles, disappearing back beneath the sand. They all lay there out of breath.

"What the hell was that thing?" Ben sat up catching his breath.

"I don't know what it was or where the hell we are but I'm not staying around here for that thing to get the munchies again," Roger said. He had one arm up and his leg rose trying to find a hold on the jagged rock face.

They climbed for an hour until they reached the top. They hauled themselves out and sat down to catch their breath.

"Where do we go now?" Sarah asked, looking around her.

"I think we'll keep walking straight ahead. I don't know where we are, but we have two suns' beating down on us. Wherever that portal took us, it sure as hell isn't Earth. Stay close together, God knows what else this nightmare land has in store for us," Ben said. He grasped Jackie's hand, and they walked off into the distance.

As they walked, the sky above darkened. A loud clap of thunder sent shivers through them; red lightning forked through the sky. They marched on until a huge forest came into view. Just then, the rain poured down with an almighty cascade.

"Into the woods now," Roger yelled, as he led the way once more.

They ran into the forest where the trees provided a lot of shelter, there was one huge tree that had its massive trunk hollowed out into a hut or cave. They sat inside, huddled together as the thunder roared. The heavy rain made it impossible to see anything outside of their hiding place. Ben rubbed his stinging, bloodshot, eyes and stared into the curtain of rain. Were his eyes deceiving him? No, something was coming toward them; it looked like a group of people.

"There's a group of people coming this way," he said.

"I can't see anything?" Sarah peered over his shoulder. The group carried spears and daggers.

"Oh, fuck," Ben whispered.

The people stopped outside the tree and gazed in at them. With them so close, anyone would realize they were not human. Thick brown matted hair covered their bodies; each one had evil yellow eyes, and blackened teeth. They were not too happy to find these invaders on their territory.

"Let's hope they're friendly," Sarah whispered.

One of them prodded Ben with a spear, the tip nicking his skin. He knocked the spear away from his body.

"What the fuck are you doing?" he screamed blood trickling from the little cut on his side.

The other beast men surrounded the tree and one dragged Ben outside by the lapel of his jacket. He stayed calm as they sniffed at him growling at each other. They pulled the others out, and three sets of weary eyes met Ben's.

"Ben, what are they doing?" Jackie asked as they sniffed at her.

"Jackie, stay calm," he whispered.

The beast men pointed their spears at the gang and tried to make them move. Ben shook his head at Jackie, Roger, and Sarah. No way, were they going anywhere with this menacing group of primitive boulder heads?

They stayed still, a beast came up to Ben growling in his face, spittle landing on his cheeks. This was the last straw for Ben. He drew his fist back punching the beast right in the mouth knocking it to the ground. The other Neanderthals stood back startled as the other one got to its feet. It roared signalling the others to close in for the kill. Roger, Jackie, and Sarah didn't know what to do, but they stayed beside Ben as these beasts attacked.

One ran at Ben with its spear pointed right at him. Ben grabbed the spear, rolled onto his back kicking his assailant over his head. He jumped to his feet with the spear in his hands. He drove it through the beast's chest; its death roar filled the air blood spurting from its mouth. Another jumped on Ben from behind, knocking him to the Ground.

Sarah picked up a heavy branch hitting the primitive things head. Her hit landed with a resounding crack. Dazed, the beast wavered on unsteady feet. Ben took the opportunity, jumping on top of it, punching its head again and again with sheer rage, his fists like hammers pounding its face to a pulp. The creature sank to the ground, but Ben was so enraged he would not stop. He was so angry he didn't realize it was dead until he saw the eyes staring lifeless to the sky.

The other beast men stared in horror at their fallen warriors, and without a backward glance, ran hollering into the forest.

Ben stood shaking with temper breathing heavy, turning to Sarah with a grin.

"Thanks Sarah, I owe you one."

He examined his bruised and bleeding knuckles.

Jackie was looking for something to wrap around his injured hands when she looked at her long sleeve T-shirt. She ripped one sleeve from the garment then ripped the sleeve in two, wrapping the strips around Ben's injured hands, she kissed him. He smiled back at her, and they walked off again in the opposite direction as the beasts.

The rain had stopped, the two suns shone down on them through the trees. They walked for what seemed like hours, but were getting nowhere fast; it appeared they were going in circles. These woods were bigger than they thought.

An uneasy feeling came over Ben. Chills swept his body and hairs stood on the back of his neck. He stopped and looked back just in time to see a beast man run behind a tree.

"We got company. Those things are following us. On the count of three, run for that opening it should take us out of here," Ben winked at Jackie. Roger and Sarah took a deep breath.

"One-two-three–run,"

They sprinted toward the edge of the forest, but the beast men were faster than them and cut them off from their exit. Three beast men stood guarding the opening snarling and growling, foam thick and white around their black lips. The gang stopped running, their breathing coming ragged and fast.

"Fuck they're fast," Roger said adjusting his glasses.

"The only way out is through them," Ben said, his eyes opening with rage. He walked toward their assailants.

They launched their spears, through the air, missing him, burying themselves in the ground on either side of him.

"Oh, that's it. You bastards are really pissing me off now," he growled to himself turning back to Roger, Sarah, and Jackie.

"I'll distract them. You run for the opening and get clear. Don't worry about me, I'll be fine,"

The beast men still stood at the exit, snarling and grimacing waiting for what he would do next. Ben pulled one spear from the ground and ran at them. The beast men attacked. They charged at him screaming and hollering with heavy tree branches for clubs. He kept running, undeterred by their weapons, he pointed the spear forwards, driving it clean through a beast's stomach and out its back. He yelled bending down to pick up the club and then went crazy hitting the other hunters over the head with a psychotic rage. Roger and the girls ran past the fight to safety. Ben was pounding skulls open like a sledgehammer to a watermelon, blood, flesh and hair covered his club when he hammered it into the ground with a scream of victory. He turned and walked away, leaving the three beasts dead, running to catch up to the others.

He caught up to them with a smile on his face still high on adrenaline after his fight and felt invincible.

They walked on without a word for a little over an hour. They were all scared. There was no way to know how many monsters inhabited this godforsaken land… or what else might lie in wait.

They came to a pathway that had six big white demon statues guarding it. The statues were huge with a wide girth and fat bellies, three on either side of the path. They stopped and looked around them.

"This seems to be the only way we can go. They're no other paths or any trails," Ben walked up the pathway followed by the others.

As they walked past the statues, their eyelids slid open and huge blood-red eyes appeared for a second before the eyes closed again.

"What the fuck?" Roger took off his glasses squinting.

"Roger what's wrong with you?" Sarah barked at him with an agitated tone.

"Those statues opened their eyes," he said with a shiver in his voice.

"That's the most idiotic thing I've ever heard," Sarah laughed.

Something moved behind her, a look of fear crossed her face that turned pale; this nightmare land was taking its toll on her nerves. A terrible grinding scraping sound came like the earth being dropped from the shovel of an excavator followed by the sound of heavy footfalls. She turned around, a scream escaping her throat. Ben and Jackie jumped with a start turning around to see what was causing the commotion. The statues had Sarah surrounded and were closing in for the kill. Stone statues that must have weighed two tonnes each were bearing down on her, ready to crush her to death.

"Fucking hell," Ben yelled, running to help her.

Roger couldn't do anything; he was stuck to the spot, his feet immobilized in something that resembled tar. He tried to get free but he couldn't move.

"Sarah," he yelled, the statues were closing in on her now, all six of them in a circle.

The statues were over nine feet tall. Ben ran at them and at the last-minute slid to the ground, his body skating between the statue's legs, he got to his knees grabbing Sarah's shoulders shaking her, she was white as a ghost, her nerves frayed, in shock because of this nightmarish world.

"Hey Sarah." he waved his hand in front of her eyes, she didn't even blink.

The statues were on top of them now, and in a rage, Ben gathered all his strength punching one with all he had. His hand crashed into it, he yelled as bone clashed with stone. He held his hand that was throbbing from the impact.

"Fuck, nice going numb nuts they're made of stone," he cursed himself.

A gap appeared between the stone giants. He lifted Sarah in his arms carrying her to safety just as a grinding bang came from behind them. He looked back and saw the stone giants had collided; now he realized why they had big bellies, like a virtual crushing room. Once they had you surrounded, they would walk in on top of you and if they had been there a second longer, they would be pancakes now.

He lay Sarah down against a tree, and then ran to help Roger get free from the stuff that glued him to the ground. The stone men were coming at them again; no matter how hard he pulled, Roger was going nowhere fast.

"Roger, take off your shoes," Ben ordered and Roger complied. He stepped out of his shoes while Ben held his arms, he was free.

"Thanks Ben," Roger spoke when Ben pushed him to the left stepping backward himself as the statues closed in again.

"God damn this place," he whispered with the statues just about on top of him now moving in a circle.

Without warning, something moved making the ground pulsate, six tentacles shot up coiling themselves around the statues with such intense force the stone cracked. The statues struggled to get free from the death embrace, the tentacles like Anaconda's, constricting, squeezing the life from them. The squid lifted them into the air and dragged them beneath the earth. Ben stood there amazed as the thing that once tried to kill him had now saved his life. Jackie was with Sarah when Ben walked back with Roger, Sarah came around.

Ben sat beside her.

"Sarah, you will be all right. You got the fright of your life that's all. You'll be fine," he glanced at Jackie.

"Let's get the fuck out of here," Sarah screamed.

"We'll be safer here until the morning comes. It will be too dark to even try to walk out of here. God knows what else is out there," Roger exclaimed as he returned to himself.

"I don't want to stay here any longer. I'm going with or without you," she screamed, walking off, the others followed her.

After they had left the pathway, not long after, a pack of dog like creatures arrived at the spot and sniffed at the air. With a loud howl, they ran into the night tracking down their prey. They had picked up our heroes' scent from the pathway and were in hot pursuit driven by hunger. The night-time hunters were on the prowl now.

The four were walking at a quick pace when a strange feeling came over Ben, his skin came out in goose bumps, and a chill ran down his spine making the hair on the back of his neck stand up, his senses told him something was close. He stopped and listened.

"Ben what's wrong?" Jackie asked with fear.

"Listen," he silenced her as he listened.

They heard nothing until the bushes behind them shook. The hair on the back of his neck stood up again to warn him of danger. He grabbed Jackie's hand and screamed. "Run,"

They sprinted as fast as they could. Behind them, the growls and footfalls of the animals echoed. There were only inches between them and the beasts; Ben pulled Jackie in front of him putting himself between her and the jaws of the things chasing them. He glanced over his right shoulder to see where the animals were, Jackie glanced back but there was nothing.

"Keep running," Ben panted as they continued to run.

The beasts had split up into two hunting packs and diverted left and right of our heroes, waiting to launch a surprise attack when they least expected it, so for now, they watched and waited in the shadows.

The four stopped running, out of breath, after another few minutes and looked back, there was still nothing. A small cliff led down to what looked like an abandoned campsite.

"All right, let's get down there before those things find us," Jackie said, climbing down with Sarah behind her.

Something moved in the darkness and Ben turned around to see what it was. He stood on the edge of the small cliff staring into the blackness never taking his eyes away. Something moved again, and out they came. Vicious dog like creatures the size of a Mini Cooper stampeded Ben, howling and barking. Ben's eyes opened wide, and before he could scream a warning, one of them jumped on him, knocking him off the fifteen-foot cliff.

The beast was right on top of him when he hit the ground; a puff of dust covered the two as they hit the bone-dry earth. The other beasts came charging down the cliff side surrounding Ben in typical predator fashion, once they had brought down their prey, the rest of the pack would join in the kill.

The creature had his arm caught in its jaws, its head shaking from side to side, trying to tear his arm from his body. He screamed as a terrible pain shot through his chest. Its claws had just ripped him open. You could see his insides with great detail; the flesh was torn open with surgical precision, in three straight lines, blood pouring from the wounds. His guts were poking through the incisions and he lost consciousness.

He clung on for dear life. A heavy rock crashed down on the beast's skull and it backed away. Roger stood there shaking with fear as the animals surrounded them. Ben was snow white, the ground around him red with his blood. The beasts gathered, and with blood curdling howls, they attacked.

Jackie cradled Ben in her arms as the beasts converged on them. The animals broke into a charge, howling and hollering, their eyes burning luminous green, jaws agape, their powerful, muscular, bodies thundering toward Jackie and the others while they stayed beside Ben. The animals leapt through the air powerful paws outstretched, sickle-like claws ready to rip and tear.

Roger and Sarah placed their arms around Jackie, waiting for the inevitable agony that would soon come. The animals were just inches away when spears and arrows rained from the sky and either hit the animals or stopped short. The beasts ran howling up the cliff face and into the darkness.

A group of people came walking out of the shadows dressed in white Roman style clothing, tunics and leather sandals. Jackie looked down at Ben, who was in agony.

"Help us. He's dying," she cried.

A tall, muscular man smiled at her, then turned to the others and said something in a language they'd never heard. Four women came to Jackie's side and looked after Ben, cleaning and bandaging his injuries. The tall man came over to Roger and Sarah and spoke.

"Do not be afraid, we mean you no harm. We are the Acunda tribe, and I'm Atari, Chief of the Acunda," he said with a little smile and spoke something else in that strange language to the other tribe members who proceeded to carry Ben off into the night.

"Come we must go now. Those creatures that attacked you are called Marigot's; their bite carries venom that can kill in a matter of hours. We must get your friend to our village if we are to save him."

"Come this way," Atari, led the way into the darkness.

For twenty minutes, they walked until they came to a big village. They took Ben to a hut where he received the medical attention he needed. For the next two hours, he slept. Jackie and the others stayed by his side until he woke. His eyes flickered and opened, his vision was a little hazy, but he got his focus back in a few seconds.

He smiled up at Jackie. "Hey," he said with a scratchy voice.

Jackie bent over and kissed him with tears in her eyes.

"Why are you crying? I will be all right now," he said, putting his arm around her.

"You could have died on me Ben. You got over one hundred fifty stitches to put you back together," she had a little wobble in her voice.

"Stitches, my ass, let's see if they know how to get us home," he sat up grimacing in pain, slowly climbing out of the bed.

"I think you should take it easy Ben. You're in no condition to walk around," Roger barked at him.

Ben looked amazed at Roger who was always quiet and never one to question him.

"You're getting more like me every day Rodge. I'd say the same thing to you in my place. Thanks for your concern, but I'm fine, okay?" he smiled at Roger who fell silent with a little blush.

He got dressed with a little help from Jackie, and both her and Roger helped him walk out to the village. The people couldn't believe he was up and walking around so fast, and they looked at him with a little fear in their eyes, thinking maybe he was a demon. Atari was sitting with the elders talking when one elder looked and pointed at Ben coming toward them, amazed at how fast he healed when only hours ago he was close to death yet here he stood with the others before them.

"You heal fast my friend," Atari looked at him in amazement.

"I know I do. Thank you and your people for saving my life and my friends. If you hadn't come along when you did, I dread to think what could have happened," Ben stopped talking when he saw the villagers staring at him. He cleared his throat and continued.

"Atari, you know we don't belong in this world, and us being here is due to being pulled into a vortex and taken from our own dimension. How do we get back?" He asked sitting with the elders. The elders debated for a while before Atari spoke.

"There is a place near to here, and there you will find what you seek. The vortex that brought you here will take you back again. It appears every three days, and the time is fast approaching. I will lead you there myself," Atari stood and walked off in front of them.

"Let's go home," Ben said leaning on Jackie and Roger as he staggered along.

They followed close behind Atari for the better part of two miles. They entered a cave and there before them was the fiery vortex that had brought them to this nightmare land. The wind howled as it did before, Atari held on to a big rock to stop himself from being dragged in as well.

"Thank you," Ben said as he was carried past him.

Atari smiled and nodded his head.

"Everyone, hold hands and don't let go," Jackie said with a smile as all four of them stepped into the swirling fiery tornado. It sealed itself shut and Atari looked with a smile.

"Goodbye my friends," he turned and left the cave.

Back inside the vortex, flames and demons flew past them as they flew through space and time at the speed of light. The vortex opened, and they fell screaming to the ground, distant echoing voices rang through Ben's mind.

*Someone shook him:*

"Wake up," it was Jackie.

Ben opened his eyes looking up at Roger, Sarah, and Jackie. He looked around him and people stood over him gazing down on him.

"Where am I," he looked around him and saw they were back at the Aces High nightclub.

"Ben, you passed out and have been out for over ten minutes. You fell down and had a seizure. You gave us all a scare," Roger helped him to a seat.

They couldn't remember the adventure they had all just had. Ben lifted his T-shirt looking at his stomach, but there were no stitches, not even a scratch! Did he dream it all when he passed out? Or was the memory of the nightmare land so intense that their minds just blocked it out? Whatever the reason, they were back now. Ben could remember everything but he kept quiet and just smiled.

"Let's go home," he said with a grin and they all walked off into the night.

As they were walking past the power generator, he spoke.

"I think we'll cross to the other side and go around the generator. It's just a feeling I have."

They crossed the road to avoid the power station.

As they were walking on the other side of the road, a bolt of lightning struck the generator sending sparks flying into the air.

"Holy fuck," Roger said, looking at Ben.

A vortex appeared for a split second and disappeared.

"How did you know?" Sarah asked with surprise in her voice. Ben looked over and laughed.

"Oh, just call it déjà vu," he took one last glance at the generator and walked on with the others.

"Thanks Atari." he whispered with a little grin.

# RISE OF THE FOUR

# THE TEMPTRESS

O n a stormy Saturday night, trouble with a capital 'T' was coming to town. A horde of bloodthirsty female vampires, were about to create havoc in the city of angels. Their leader, who looked like a twenty-eight-year-old sex Goddess, was awakened from her resting place by a cult of satanic morons eight weeks earlier.

They had heard stories of an ancient vampire queen, lying dormant in a hidden crypt somewhere in the Angeles Forest. Their so-called high priest had done all his research and narrowed the area down to a within a hundred-meter radius right in the middle of the forest. Armed with this new knowledge they made their plans to find the crypt and discover for themselves if these legends were true or just mere fiction.

Their big night arrived and they met at the forest at ten o' clock. The place was closed but that wasn't going to deter these clowns. Climbing over a chained barrier they walked into the forest, flash lights illuminating their way as their leader studied the crude map he had drawn, after a while they were right in the middle of the forest, he looked up then back at his map.

"This is the place," he said with excitement.

He slung a backpack from his shoulder unzipping it, he extracted an old leather-bound book and placed it on the ground as the others collected twigs and branches to get a fire started. Once the fire was burning, they all sat in a circle around it.

"It's time to begin." The leader said opening the book to the middle pages he had marked and began to read the ancient Sumerian text that he barely understood how to translate. In a booming voice he recited the text, but unbeknownst to him, he was reading the wrong passage. A stiff breeze stirred up making the flames in the fire dance and sway a cold chill ran down their spines yet the man continued his recitation. A few feet from where they were performing the ritual, eight-feet underground lay a stone Sarcophagus and inside lay a decaying, emaciated female body, arms crossed upon her chest, her skeletal face twisted and rancid, with worms and maggots crawling from her nasal cavity, cheeks and mouth. Suddenly her eyes shot open, glowing luminous blue in the darkness, she turned her head left and right with the bones and tendons squeaking and cracking, she unfolded her arms and turned her wretched head sharply to the right, vomited up a disgusting blue green liquid that had maggots and worms writhing within the vile soup. Her mouth opened wide and huge triangular teeth cut through her top and bottom gums, after all these centuries of confinement she was very hungry and needed to feed. The vampire's super sharp hearing picked up a voice right above her, she was too weak to break free from her tomb as her body had wasted away, but her telepathic powers were still strong. She lay still eyes open wide she concentrated hard falling into a trance. Above ground, the leader finished his incantation looking around him.

"What a crock of shit," he said casting the book onto the fire. They laughed cracking open cans of beer. As they sat drinking, the vampire found her mark. One of the men dropped his beer, standing, he walked in a trance to where the monster waited.

He stood there motionless, arms by his side. He spoke to some invisible force beside him.

"Yes, I understand," he moaned and walked a little bit away, dropping to his knees he started using his hands to dig, faster and faster he dug until his finger-tips were bloodied and before long he found what he was searching for. There in the dirt was an ancient blade, rusted but still razor sharp. He walked back to where Stephanie waited to be set free. The rest of his friends joined him wondering what the hell was going on.

"Hey Devon, what are you doing?" one of them asked finishing off his beer. Devon said nothing but dropped to his hands and knees, placing the blade to his throat he slit himself open and gagged as his blood seeped into the ground. They tried to get the blade away from him but he pushed them away and with a fearful cry drove the blade right through his neck collapsing on top of the vampire's tomb, the blood poured out but seemed to vanish into the ground without leaving a stain or anything.

The rest of the group swallowed hard as fear took hold and one of them turned on their so-called leader.

"This is all your fault, you and your damn book."

Below ground, the slain man's blood dripped onto the vampire, and as if by magic, flowed upward to her mouth. As she tasted the blood something began to happen, she began to regenerate, the flesh growing back on her left hand. With a shriek she pounded the stone cap of her prison and it moved, she gave it another shove and dislodged it completely only to be greeted by a mound of earth above her.

As the Satanists argued, her hands shot through the ground grabbing hold of the dead man's body pulling it under. The others turned and started running. The body shot out of the ground through the air landing with a thump minus its head. Her arms appeared again as she hoisted herself free from the confines of her prison, she saw the fire but nobody around. She sniffed at the air and hissed, running at super human speed into the night.

They had awakened Stephanie, a three-hundred-year-old vampire queen and she was now hunting them down one by one. Everything about her was built for the kill, super human speed, strength, agility, heightened senses, night vision and the ability to fly, she was the perfect predator. As the panicked Satanists ran, she came rushing from the shadows knocking one of them to the ground. He screamed when she mounted him pinning his arms down, her emaciated naked body felt like ice upon his chest, in the pale moonlight he saw her face as she leered down on him.

"You have awakened me from my ancient slumber and freed me from my prison. For that I thank you, but I'm afraid as a man you must die," she opened her mouth and his eyes opened wide with fear as those triangular teeth grew from her gums and she hissed sinking those horrible fangs into his flesh, ripping a gaping hole in his throat, far from the classic vampire puncture marks in the movies, and blood sprayed like a burst water main, dripping from her face as she drained him of every drop.

She sat up licking the blood from her lips, and some flesh grew back on her bones, her breasts filled out and ebony black hair sprouted from her scalp. She stood looking into the darkness, and with one big jump she took to the sky. Before long she spied the remaining men as they neared the barrier. With an ear-piercing scream she dove from the sky right towards them and as the vampire flew past two of the men stood there gagging and choking, blood pouring from the ragged gashes on their throats. She landed grabbing one by the hair pulling his head back followed by a sucking slurping sound as she drained him of his blood. The body fell to the ground and she stood almost fully regenerated apart from some flesh missing from her legs and left side of her face. Stephanie knelt beside the second man ripping his throat open she slurped his blood and when she was done, the moonlight shone upon her and she looked beautiful now. Then from the shadows the man in black appeared.

"Welcome back to the land of the living dear daughter," he smiled.

She hissed at him, her eyes burning red with rage.

"You left me locked in that vile pit for nearly two-hundred and fifty years, and done nothing to help me. Now all you can say is welcome back to the land of the living?" Satan smiled.

"I have helped you daughter, who do you think sent these morons to awaken you? I need you now my beautiful seductress, for the guardians of the final gateway have been united and I need you destroy them." He stopped when she laughed.

"It's typical of you isn't it father? For years you leave me rot, then when you want something, you bring me back. These guardians must be a handful if the mighty Satan cannot defeat them by himself," she gave a wry grin.

"Do not antagonize me daughter or you will find yourself in a place much worse than the vile pit you just escaped from, and the word suffering will have a whole new meaning for you, do I make myself clear." He barked, just then a car engine started up and the sound of screeching tires broke the silence. Stephanie hissed looking in the direction of the car.

"Don't worry about them daughter, I have more important work for you, but you cannot do it alone you will need some help," Satan waited for her to reply.

Don't worry about that father, I will recruit some strong women and turn them to the ways of the vampire. These guardians of yours where do I find them?" He nodded his head with a grin.

"Excellent daughter, these are the four I want you to destroy," he waved his hand and the air began to shimmer and from the shimmering, faces appeared. Those of the four heroes. One by one they rotated and she put them to memory. It stopped on Ben and Satan became enraged at the sight of him.

"This bastard is the one I want taken out more than the others my daughter, for he is the leader of the four. Do not underestimate him for he is much stronger than you think, though I doubt even he will be able to resist you my beautiful Stephanie," he smiled at her.

"This should be easy enough, he's a man and there's only one thing men want. First, I'll seduce him, then fuck him before I destroy him," Her naked body shuddered in the moonlight as she thought of the fun that was to come.

"I'll leave you to do your thing daughter. I'll take care of my so-called worshippers that left so hastily. Do not disappoint me Stephanie, for your own sake," he walked into the night and vanished in a cloud of smoke.

Stephanie stood there, the images of the four still going around in her mind. The one called Ben is her target and she will make him suffer for she hates men, and believes men should be the servants of women, not women serving men. She will make sure that women rule this world and men made their slaves to do as they command, and if they disobey death will be swift.

As the car sped down the road, Satan suddenly appeared in front of it. He was in black so they didn't see him standing there until the last second. Satan turned his hands palm up and they erupted into flame. He clapped them together and a wall of fire raced towards the car. The occupants screamed as the driver turned the wheel sharply in a panic, and sent the car off the road tumbling down an embankment. It came to rest on its roof, smoke rising from under the hood. Satan appeared beside the wreck and bent down to look inside, and just smiled at the carnage before him. Three of the passengers were dead.

"Oh, you should have been wearing your seatbelts," he grinned. The driver coughed and gagged and the prince of darkness walked slowly around to his side, placed his hands on his knees bent over and gazed in. The man was a mangled mess with his legs so badly broken they were twisted and distorted with the bones sticking out through the flesh. He trembled as he made eye contact with Satan.

"Help me, please," he whimpered.

Satan looked surprised.

"Me help you, oh my dear boy why would I want to help a pathetic insect like you. But I'll tell you what I'll do, I can make your suffering go away. You'd like that wouldn't you?" he mocked the injured man, but he was in so much agony he slowly nodded his head.

"Very well, since you were kind enough to help me tonight, consider this my reward to you," he stood and walked away whistling to himself. He turned around his hands ablaze and let loose a wall of flame engulfing the car, screams of agony came from within until the fuel tank exploded with a thunderous ka-boom sending smoke and flames into the air.

Satan stood there, hands behind his back smiling as the car burned, the flames glinting in his black lifeless eyes, then he snorted and erupted into laughter.

"Help me. Oh, that's one I shall never forget. A mere mortal asking me, the mighty Satan for help. Ah well, after all the bastard Jehovah did make them in his own image, what do you expect from such pathetic loser of a so-called God." And with a flash and puff of smoke he was gone.

♦

For the next five weeks, Stephanie's thirst for blood was insatiable. Men were such easy victims. They all had only one thing on their minds, Sex. Once they were under her influence, they would follow her to Hell if she wanted them to do so. In the back allies' things would get hot, as the guy tried to get her to open her legs, she would laugh evilly. One night a guy got more than he wanted when Stephanie dropped her hand down and crushed his balls, enjoying seeing him in pain.

"You men are all so pathetic and weak. I'm amazed that they call this a man's world. Well, not for much longer," she whispered, her pointed teeth ripping into his throat.

The more blood she took, the more beautiful she became. Her spell worked on women just as effectively but for the women, her bite was an orgasmic taste of heaven, turning her female lovers into her vampire sisters. And so, it began, twenty-three female vampires and the vampire queen had arrived in town, bringing with them the temptation of sex, suffering and death.

At the Aces High, Ben was out without Jackie. She had gone for a week on a business trip and wouldn't be back for another two days. He missed her terribly, so rather than being stuck at home, he headed out for the night. He stood at the bar drinking his beer, then he saw a lot of scantily dressed women come through the doors. He looked away with no interest. No man in the nightclub could keep his eyes off them. The women were on the dance floor, dirty dancing, and flirting with the patrons. Ben looked at them, disgusted with their behaviour.

"At least my Jackie isn't like that," he said to himself walking to the Gents. On his way out, he bumped into a woman. She was six feet tall, with shoulder length black hair, her dark green eyes made her look irresistible, not to mention her short leather mini skirt, and black thigh high leather boots. Ben walked past her, but she followed him back to the bar. She stood beside him and winked with a smile. He took his glass and walked away shaking his head disapprovingly at her flirtatious behaviour. She looked puzzled by Ben's lack of interest, most men would kill to be with her, but Ben had no interest. He was sitting in the corner when she walked over and sat beside him.

Her green eyes stared into his and a strange feeling came over him as she cast her spell. If Ben wouldn't be seduced, she would put him in a trance and make him do as she pleased. She licked her lips seductively and he became uncontrollably attracted to her now. His eyes fixed on her his heart beating faster; he swallowed hard when she smiled again.

"I'm Stephanie," she said with a smile, holding out her hand.

"And I'm Ben," he said shaking it.

Her smile turned into a frown when she realized Ben was fighting her hypnotic mind games. He stepped back, shook his head, snapping back to reality.

"I'm sorry. I'm already taken and I will do nothing to hurt her," he walked away from a furious Stephanie.

She was amazed by Ben's strength and loyalty and she admired that in him. Maybe men were not all as bad as she had thought. She saw her sisters trying it on with Ben and telepathically, she warned them to leave him alone. They backed off and mingled with the other patrons.

For the rest of the night, he kept his distance sitting alone. He thought to himself; "What was that woman trying to do to me? Why did I feel attracted to her when I wanted nothing to do with her? Could I have been hypnotized?"

He was beating himself up and couldn't take another minute of being in the same place with these women. Best he left, he decided, no matter how lonely home would be without Jackie. He walked toward the door when Stephanie approached him again. Gritting his teeth, he gave her a stern look and spoke

"Look. I'm telling you now and for the last time. I'm spoken for and engaged to be married. I don't cheat and I don't mess around, okay? Now please leave me alone," he turned and stormed out.

Stephanie stood there smiling, amazed that Ben rejected her remained a bolt from the blue to her.

"You can only resist me for so long, Ben. You will be mine," she said to herself as her eyes turned to violet, the sign of vampire lust.

Meanwhile, her vampire sisters were making men dance to their tune, kissing them and touching them, driving them crazy. Stephanie gazed at her sisters and sent them a silent message:

"Kill these insufferable morons, they don't deserve you, my sisters."

With her orders being followed, she walked out of the nightclub, her appetite was getting to her, and she needed to feed. A man came up to her, trying to get lucky, he slipped an arm around her, kissing her, while his other hand fondled her breasts. Stephanie just smiled at the poor idiot and led him to a back alley. She laughed as the guy tried to force her legs open, but stopped in a rage insulted by Stephanie's laughter. She put her hand around his throat and choked him.

"You're so pathetic, you don't know how to love a woman, and you men only want one thing. You're nothing but a pig, now let's see if you bleed like one?" She hissed her eyes turning red, her teeth became elongated.

She tore the flesh from his neck, making blood squirt all over her face and drained him of every drop. She walked casually from the alley licking her lips, her hunger satisfied.

Ben lay in bed restless. He tossed and turned growing more irritable by the second. He sat up, reached for his cigarettes then headed down the stairs to the back door. He stood there smoking, the vision of Stephanie; her dark green eyes, long flowing black hair, ruby-red lip, her alluring smile, all flashed through his mind.

"Why can't I stop thinking about you?" he asked himself crushing out his cigarette going back to bed. He fell asleep easy this time.

In his dreams, he could hear Stephanie calling his name as if she was in the room with him.

"You can't resist me forever. Give in to me Ben and let me fulfil your sexual desires."

He sat up in the bed, sweat dripping down his face. He felt a draft coming from the window. The net curtains were fluttering in the midnight breeze.

"I don't remember opening the window,"

He climbed out of bed to investigate.

Stephanie was in vampire form now and she floated in the air looking at Ben's semi naked body as he pulled in the window. Before he drew the curtains, he looked to his right, left and then straight ahead, staring in Stephanie's direction, who was looking right back at him from behind a tree. He drew the curtains and went back to bed.

After half an hour, she tapped on his window softly calling out...

"Ben, let me in, I don't want to hurt you; I want to show you the pleasures I have to give you. Let me in," she whispered floating in the air outside the bedroom window.

He appeared at the window, a blank expression on his face like he was in a trance and opened it. Stephanie landed beside him; he took her in his arms kissing her. She let her short skirt drop to the floor and pulled off her top. She took his hands, let them feel her huge breasts, they were bigger than Jackie's.

"Make love to me Ben," she whispered in his ear as her teeth became pointed, but she would not bite him.

He carried her to the bed and for the next four hours, he made love to her. She dressed herself after they finished and left through the window again. She had to be back to her lair before dawn.

Ben woke with a jump; from what he thought was a nightmare.

"What the fuck?" He breathed heavily looking around the room in a panic.

He couldn't remember a thing. To him it was just an erotic dream... but it was so real. He'd been unable to resist her. He got dressed and walked down the stairs to the kitchen sitting there in a daze trying to figure out what had just happened to him.

"Why am I dreaming of another woman? It's Jackie that I love and cherish. Why is Stephanie haunting my dreams when I have no interest in her?" he was miserable now.

He couldn't bear the thought of cheating on Jackie. Did he really make love to Stephanie or was it all a dream? He didn't know.

It was now eight in the morning and the sun was blazing. He was in the kitchen making coffee and listening to the radio when the news came on and scared him to death.

"This is Cindy Shields reporting live from down town L.A. Early this morning the bodies of eight young men were found completely drained of their blood, gaping wounds on the side of their necks appear to be vampiric in fashion and police psychologists are calling it the work of a crazed vampire fanatic whose psychotic vampire fantasies, are driving him to murder. Police have several people in custody and they are helping with their inquiries. Will this vampire freak strike again? Has Dracula taken up residency here in Los Angeles? Nobody knows. While this maniac is roaming our streets, no one will be safe. This is Cindy Shields for A-B-C-7. News,"

Ben reached over and turned off the radio. He stood there thinking when there was a knock on the door. He opened it and Roger stood there with his umbrella as it was raining hard.

"Hey Rodge, what brings you here in this weather? The kettles just boiled if you fancy a cuppa," Ben said, closing the door behind him.

"I'd love one mate," Roger followed him to the kitchen.

Ben made Roger's coffee and handed him the mug.

"Did you hear the news this morning?

"About the bodies drained of blood with the bite marks?" Roger asked with a grin.

Ben frowned.

"That's the one. It's freaky to think someone thinks he's a vampire, so much so he's drinking people's blood,"

"It takes all kinds to make the world go around I suppose. When is Jackie coming back?" Roger asked, sipping his coffee.

"She'll be back tomorrow, but I'm missing her," Ben replied as he thought about the dream he had of Stephanie.

"Roger, can I ask you a silly question?" He was sure he looked a little more than embarrassed.

"You know you can talk to me about anything," Roger replied, sitting up attentively.

"Last night I was at the Aces High, some women were there acting like complete little tarts. Anyway, one of them tried it on with me and I turned and walked away. She followed me all over the place and at one point when I looked in her eyes, I felt very uncomfortable, like I was under her spell. But, to cut a long story short, I came home in a taxi at around twelve thirty and went to bed. I couldn't sleep at all. Her voice and her face kept going through my head so I got up for a smoke trying to relax. I went back to bed and fell asleep, but I had the strangest dream, she was in the room with me and we had sex for hours. Then the sun beamed through the window. I feel miserable that I could be dreaming of another woman when I love Jackie so much. Is that cheating Roger, to dream of someone else and make love to them? It seemed so real I feel guilty for even dreaming it."

Ben looked worried, he was pale, and felt a little sick. Roger just laughed, placing his hand on Ben's shoulder.

"Ben, I don't know what to say mate. All I can tell you is this, you can't cheat on someone just by having a wet dream, and that's all it was, a silly little dream. Now go to bed, get a little rest and stop beating yourself up about it okay? Sarah and I both know how committed you are to Jackie, and how you would never hurt her. Give yourself a break man, go to bed and you'll feel better later. I'll let myself out." Roger said with a smile, gently closing the front door behind him.

Ten minutes later, the phone rang while Ben was in the shower. He came out in his bathrobe and saw the light flashing on the answering machine. He pressed the button and waited.

"Next message received today at ten-oh-five am,"

Hey, baby. It's me, just calling to say I love you and I miss you. I'll be home tomorrow and can't wait to see you. Bye, love you," The message ended. Ben smiled, walking up the stairs to lie down for a while.

On the outskirts of town, inside a deep cave the vampires slept, waiting for the sun to set. Stephanie opened her eyes, whispered, "Ben," and smiled.

Even in his sleep, he could hear her calling his name.

"Stephanie, what do you want from me?" He moaned.

Her voice echoed in his mind again.

"I want you, Ben."

He woke up, jumped out of the bed, and hurriedly got dressed. He ran down the stairs with a cigarette in his mouth, grabbed his car keys, and stormed out. His beloved Mustang thundered down the road and the heavy metal sound of W.A.S.P. filled the car as he drove. Why was Stephanie in his mind? He didn't know, but he knew now that last night wasn't a dream, he heard her call his name, and say she wanted him. He knew from the old horror movies that vampires were the only creatures that could do that.

He stopped outside an electrical store and bought a video camera and memory card. If Stephanie was to return tonight, he would have the evidence. He drove home and started work placing the video camera out of sight in the bedroom.

"Jackie I'm so sorry for this baby, but I didn't know what was happening," he said with tears in his eyes. It was now a little after six the sun was quickly setting.

Inside the cave, the vampires woke. Their faces twisted into a frightening yawn, their eyes were bright red, their teeth elongated. Stephanie appeared beside them.

"Come, my sisters, night is falling. It is time to feed," she screamed as they floated off the ground flying from the cave at incredible speed.

Two young men were walking into town when they heard the vampires laugh. They glanced up at the sky and saw three vampires flying down at them. They screamed, trying to run, but were lifted off the ground, into the air and drained of their blood, bodies falling back to earth with a bang.

Ben lay in his bed. He could see and hear Stephanie through the window. Her red eyes and pointed canines smiled at him.

"Ben, open the window and let me in," she tapped on the glass and he went into a trance. The video camera recorded everything. The window opened and like before Stephanie undressed, he took her in his arms and made love to her. Her eyes became violet, her breathing got heavy, and her mouth opened wide, teeth ready to bite. She sank her fangs into his neck and he moaned.

He woke with a start as the sun came through the window.

"What?" he looked at his watch; six thirty in the morning.

"Not again." He ran to the video camera and with trembling hands brought it down to the sitting room. Using the cords that came with the camera, he connected it up to the television dreading what he would see.

He sat on the sofa with the remote control and pushed the play button, there he was lying asleep in bed. He forwarded the recording and pressed play again. He saw himself getting out of bed, opening the window and there floating in the air was Stephanie. With growing trepidation, he watched as Stephanie came into the room and they climbed into bed together. Ben closed his eyes for a moment and when he re-opened them, Stephanie was kissing his neck in the video.

The sounds of a car pulling into the driveway startled him. He stopped the recording and went to the window, through the curtains he watched Jackie get out of a taxi.

He ran to the front door and swallowed hard.

"How am I going to explain all this to Jackie," he thought as she ran to him throwing her arms around him.

"I missed you so much Ben," she kissed him.

"I missed you too. This has been the longest week I have ever had in my life," he picked up her suitcases.

She walked through the door, glancing into the sitting room and saw the video camera sitting on the coffee table.

"What's with the video camera?" she asked with a puzzled look on her face and a raised eyebrow.

"Oh boy, If Stephanie doesn't kill me, Jackie will," he thought to himself taking a deep breath and following Jackie to the kitchen.

"Jackie, something happened while you were gone. I'll explain everything in a while, but we need Roger and Sarah," he picked up the phone, dialled and Roger answered.

"It's true Rodge; I have it all on tape. We have a vampire problem that's got to be sorted out. Now, you and Sarah get the hell over here," he slammed down the phone.

Jackie heard Ben talking to Roger.

"Ben what's been going on since I left? Did I hear you say vampires?" she asked with a serious look on her face.

"Yes, you heard right Jackie, female vampires at least twenty of them. I saw them at the Aces High and I knew they were trouble, but now I'm convinced that these bitches are responsible for at least ten murders in the past two days," he sat down letting out a long sigh.

"And how do you know they're vampire's Ben?" Jackie was getting angry.

"Because their leader Stephanie has been haunting me and taunting me the past two nights, I can hear her in my head and it's like she's in the room with me," he was nervous now as he saw Jackie getting madder by the minute.

"The bitch, how dare she try to take my man from me? I don't care how many fucking vampires are with her, I swear I'll put a stake through her heart myself," she yelled as a knock came to the front door. Jackie stormed from the sitting room to answer it with temper.

"Come in," she roared at Roger and Sarah slamming the door behind them.

"What's going on with you two?" Sarah asked, looking at a furious Jackie.

"Roger, remember that conversation we had yesterday. It wasn't a dream. That bitch was here last night, and it looks like I was in a trance. I have it on tape," Ben pressed play on the video camera.

The only thing they saw was Ben getting out of bed and opening the window. There was no evidence of Stephanie. The tape was playing, and it seemed like Ben was talking to himself until Stephanie laughed, and the tape went blank, Ben pressed rewind and forward but the film was blank.

"She was here I swear she was." he stopped and took a deep breath.

Jackie saw the bite on his neck and looked at him.

"Ben did that bitch bite you?" she asked with temper.

"What bite?" he ran to the mirror looking at his neck.

"Oh fuck. That's it. This bitch is going down," he barked.

"And where do we find her?" Jackie asked with a smart Alec grin.

"If she's into me, she'll be back tonight for another bite, and when she does you lot will wait for her with pointed stakes and drive them right through her black heart," he replied with venom in his voice.

That evening as the sun set, Ben lay in bed with Jackie, Roger, and Sarah hiding in the closet. For what seemed like hours, they waited, until they heard a tapping on the window.

"Ben, let me in," Stephanie whispered, he slowly got out of the bed and walked in a trance to the window opening it.

Stephanie floated in, landing beside him. She was just about to bite him when a light switched on and there stood Jackie, Roger, and Sarah.

"Get away from my man you bitch," Jackie screamed.

Stephanie laughed and grinned, showing her pointed teeth.

"He belongs to me now," she hissed walking towards Jackie.

"You're one ugly-looking bitch," Jackie screamed, raising the stake above her head ready to plunge it into Stephanie's heart.

Stephanie's strength was unreal, and she threw Jackie across the room. She turned to Roger, hissing as she punched him, sending him crashing against the wall. Sarah attacked, but Stephanie swung around and slapped her, knocking her out, cold.

She walked back to Ben and kissed him.

"Come with me my lover," she held out her hand.

Jackie got to her feet and jumped on Stephanie's back.

"He's mine, bitch," she screamed ripping Stephanie's hair.

Jackie's voice echoed through his head and Ben snapped out of the trance, as Stephanie turned around, he punched her twice in the mouth sending her staggering backwards. She tasted her own blood and licked her split lip, spitting on the ground, Ben stood there with his fists clenched, breathing heavy.

She hissed at him.

"Why, Ben? You were the only man I ever loved. Why would you do this?" she asked, looking sad hanging her head to her chest, a little tear slid down her cheek.

While she stood there in her moment of sorrow, Jackie crept up behind her with the stake held high above her head; teeth clenched in sheer rage and plunged the stake through Stephanie's back. Her mouth opened wide, and she screamed. She turned to Jackie trying to claw at her face. Roger attacked plunging his stake into her chest and she spat black blood on the floor. Her screams were unreal, as she turned around, Ben punched her again, then caught her head and turned it to the left with a loud crack as her neck broke, her head lolled to her left shoulder, but she was still standing. She reached up her hands, grabbed her head, and with one jerk and crack placed it back on turning her head left and right as her bones cracked and squeaked.

Jackie took Sarah's stake and plunged it straight through Stephanie's heart. The vampire queen smouldered and blistered and she screamed.

In the cave, her sisters ran screaming around thrashing their arms through the air as they also began to burn. Stephanie's screams were nerve-racking as she erupted in a ball of flame, only a pile of ashes remained on the floor. The vampires were gone.

While Ben and Roger were helping Sarah to her feet, a big red glow flew from the ashes across the room into Jackie's body, and she became rigid like a statue, breathing hard before her eyes turned to violet the sign of vampire lust. Stephanie was in Jackie's body now.

"Are you all right Jackie?" Ben asked, coming over to her.

She threw her arms around him, kissing him.

"I feel great, my lover. In fact, I feel born again," she said with a smile.

They walked back down to the kitchen and sat at the table. Jackie's eyes turned from blue to green as Stephanie appeared.

"I love you Ben and now I'm with you always," she whispered with a smile before she disappeared.

Stephanie and Jackie were now one. The woman he loved was also the woman he hated. But Stephanie doesn't care, she wants to be with him and being inside of Jackie is the only way she can be close to the only man she ever loved.

# HARRY GORDON'S FINAL RAMPAGE

✠

Three months passed since Harry Gordon escaped from the asylum, vanishing without a trace, leaving behind only a dead security guard and his huge footprints. He hasn't gone too far. He's coming back one last time to finish what he started, only this time without the chainsaw. His hatred for the four young people has become even stronger, an obsession now. Nothing else mattered to him, but their demise at his will. When Harry lost his saw three months earlier, he also lost his immortality. The power of the metal kept him alive, and without it, he can now die. But he didn't care, as long as they died before him, it was okay.

Once again, he will disrupt their lives and make them pay in blood for what they did to him. They had better watch out because Harry is back with a bloodthirsty vengeance.

It's late at night and a middle-aged man is walking down a dreary road after his car broke down a few miles away. The Moonlight illuminated the dark clouds that prevented its heavenly rays from breaking through to light up the darkness. He stumbled into a puddle of water left by the torrential rain the earlier night.

"Goddammit," he exclaimed, shaking the water off his shoes.

As he walked on, the trees swayed back and forth, leaves fluttering as a cold December wind broke the silence of the night. The man turned up the collar on his winter coat, placed his hands in his pockets, walking on at a fast pace trying to keep warm.

As he turned a corner, a huge figure blocked his path. The wind whistled through the trees and Harry laughed to himself. The frightened man looked at him.

"What do you want? Who are you?" he backed away from the figure approaching him. Terror crossed his face, he gasped for breath, trying to swallow as Harry towered over him. The man screamed, raising his arms to defend himself as an axe slashed through the air amputating one of his arms then buried itself in the top of his skull.

The body lay on the ground, its twinging nerves throwing it into convulsions. Twigs snapped in half as Harry pushed his way through the woods, soft earth compressing under his heavy footsteps. A beam of moonlight broke through the trees and lit up his twisted, distorted face, which then disappeared back into the blackness of the woods.

His left arm hung by his side; the axe gripped in his huge hand. He marched on until he came to a stop behind a house.

The house was big, with a huge back garden that was lavishly decorated with a variety of colourful flowers around the borders, and in the middle of the garden was a lit up three tier fountain. Harry breathed heavy as through the kitchen window, he could see a figure moving.

The house belonged to a seventy-four-year-old widow, Catherine Morrison. She was a kind old lady, and well liked in the town. Catherine was only five foot one tall and frail, but she always had a smile for everyone. She'd been living on her own for over twenty-five years since her husband Richard passed away, after suffering from an inoperable brain tumour. Towards the end, he couldn't even remember who Catherine was or why she was in his house. But Catherine was a staunch old girl, and she stuck in there right until his final days.

Her two sons, William and Richard were money hungry men. They tried to get her to go into a nursing home because it was too dangerous for her to be alone. But Catherine laid it down the line for them both.

"I told the two of you before, this is my home, and I will not be leaving it. It will be my home until the day I die. It will be here and not in some God forsaken old folk's home I will live out my last days. Now go, leave me alone. The only thing you two ever loved was money." She slammed the door behind them.

Little did she know, her wish of dying in the house was about to come true.

She was sitting down watching TV drinking her herbal tea when there was a loud knock at her front door. She put the cup and saucer on the small coffee table turning down the volume. She stood and walked to the door. She couldn't see anyone through the glass, and as she neared the door, the loud knock came again.

"Who is it? Who's there?" she asked.

Harry stood back from the door.

"There's been a terrible accident. Someone's dead," he said with a horrible grin, raising the axe above his head. The door latch clicked, she opened it.

"Who's dead?" Catherine asked, opening the door all the way.

"You are, bitch!" Harry yelled, bringing the axe down on her arm amputating it coarsely. The severed limb dangled from the door handle. The woman screamed in agony. Blood gushing from the wound, a nub of bone and tattered flesh is all that remained of her arm, which had been amputated at the elbow.

She screamed, trying to get to the kitchen where she had her panic button. She staggered towards the kitchen door with the hulking figure of Harry grinning at the doorway. She got to the kitchen and locked the door before she became weak from the loss of blood and shock.

The door was in splinters as Harry kicked his way through it. The woman screamed and cried, trying to get to her feet. The panic button lay on the worktop by the sink and she wobbled toward it. Harry struck her with the axe again, this time in the left leg and she fell to the floor, her leg buckling from the blow, bones shattering with a sickening crack. The tears ran down her face as she tried to back away from him.

"Leave me alone, please. Why are you hurting me like this?" she yelled when he reached her.

Her pain wracked body shivering with shock. Harry looked like a giant as she glanced up at him. She wanted to talk, but fear kept her silent. As he stood there, with the axe above his head ready to bring it down on the terrified old woman, he stopped and lowered it.

A kitchen knife lay on the counter. With his free hand, he reached over and grabbed it, his mutilated face twisted into a gruesome grin as he knelt on one knee beside her. He stared into her tear filled, frightened eyes. His eyes burned with an evil rage, for in his twisted, psychotic mind, he didn't see an old woman, he saw Jackie, the one who humiliated him by cutting him up with his own saw, he lost a fight to a woman, and that was one humiliation too far. His hatred for her was so unreal.

He yelled, "You bitch," pulling the knife's blade across her throat. Her body went into convulsions, blood pouring from her severed neck across the floor. Harry went crazy. He held the knife over his head plunging it into her body again and again. He pulled the knife from her chest to belly button splitting her open like a gutted fish. He stood up, raised the axe above his head, and hacked the body to pieces, laughing all the while. Body parts and little morsels of flesh covered the floor, blood painted the walls and Harry's face. He walked through the back door, leaving behind a butchered mess. Into the night, he went axe and knife by his side and a smile across his face.

Dawn broke, and the sky had turned into an orange-red colour as the sun rose over the distant hills. Harry Gordon was a mere silhouette walking farther and farther away. A day later, he was only a mile from town.

Edward Miles was the cemetery caretaker. He had been the caretaker for the last seventeen years and he started work at six in the morning. Edward wasn't mentally all there, he was slightly autistic, but he was a good grounds keeper. He was in his late fifties, his baldhead, and ageing, wrinkled skin made him look like someone from an old Frankenstein movie. He was just opening the gates, when Harry appeared behind him, putting the axe on the ground, he crept up on Edward. He lifted the man high into the air and slammed him down on the spikes across the top of the gate. The spikes penetrated through his stomach and chest and blood spurted from his mouth. His arms and legs shook and trembled for a while before they flopped down and hung motionless. The gates creaked open and closed with a clash as a small wind whistled through the cemetery.

Harry walked on for another two hours before he came to a small wooded area. He stopped and looked around before he entered. He remembered it from the last time he was here. He stomped through the thick bushes before he saw a house and stopped dead in his tracks, it was Jackie's.

His breathing became heavy, and he gripped the axe. His eyes went wild as through the trees he could see Ben in the kitchen filling the kettle and Jackie sitting reading a book. Harry thought back to the night Ben kicked his ass and how Jackie butchered him with his own saw and his rage flared. He was tempted to barge in and kill them at once, but he quelled his anger and smiled as he thought of the things, he would do to them. How he was going to make them scream and bleed.

Ha! Little did he know what waited for him? For inside Jackie was the spirit of Stephanie! The vampire queen and anyone dared try to hurt Jackie, she would make them suffer.

Ben and Jackie sat talking and laughing while they listened to the radio. Ben looked at Jackie as she smiled, and the memory of how close he came to losing her flashed through his mind. She put her coffee down on the table and gripped his hand.

"Hey, are you okay?" he took a deep breath.

"Yes, I'm fine, just thinking that's all," He replied, standing up from the table, walking to the sink pouring his coffee down the drain.

He didn't see Jackie's eyes turn from blue to green as Stephanie appeared with a smile. She disappeared back into Jackie again after a few seconds, she walked over to Ben. He was just standing at the sink staring out the window into the woods. He couldn't forget the night Gordon came back. If he only knew, Harry was looking right back at him from the cover of the trees. Jackie put her arms around him and rested her head on his shoulder.

"Penny for your thoughts," she whispered in his ear.

He tried to fake a smile and spoke

"It was nothing, only old memories."

He put his arms around her and kissed her. Inside his mind, he was reliving the night she almost died. The roar of the chainsaw, the blood, the tears, and every detail was clear in his mind, and then there was Stephanie. He hated himself for that incident. They stood there in a loving embrace when there was a loud knock at the door.

"I'll get it," she whispered, kissing him on the cheek. She walked to the door and opened it.

Roger and Sarah rushed past her. Jackie didn't have time to speak as they disappeared into the kitchen.

"Well, good morning to you too Jackie," she said to herself with a little smile closing the door. She walked back to the kitchen.

A serious look marred Ben's face as she appeared in the doorway. She looked at him, then at Roger and Sarah.

"What's going on you all look so serious," she stood beside Ben, who had his arms folded across his chest, his facial expression deadly serious now as he glanced over at Roger.

"Do you want to tell her Roger?" he said, clenching his teeth in anger.

Jackie looked worried now.

"Ben what is it? What's going on," she asked with a tremor in her voice. Roger swallowed hard taking a deep breath.

"Jackie you better sit down," he pulled out a chair. She sat beside him.

"Jackie. There have been three murders in the past two days. The bodies were found not far from here. The way they were killed was brutal and vicious. The cops are looking for the killer as we speak and they have a good idea of who is responsible," Roger stopped and looked at Ben.

He turned away to look out the kitchen window into the wooded area. Harry was staring right back at him grinning a horrible grin waving at Ben and laughing to himself as he found his little game to be hysterical. He stood up and danced around a tree laughing his head off, waving his arms above his head, waving them around like a lunatic, enjoying the fact that Ben couldn't see him, but he could see Ben. Harry fell down breathless from laughing and grabbed a hold of his axe again. He stood up, tears still in his eyes from the laughter as he thought of how they would scream and bleed and die by his hand. He ran his thumb along the axes blade and smiled. "Oh, it won't be long now," he growled hugging the axe to his chest grinning.

Back inside Jackie was waiting to hear who the killer was.

"Roger, tell me," She yelled her voice whimpering with anxiety.

Ben breathed heavily, his temper rising.

"They think it was... Harry Gordon," Sarah spoke the terrifying words.

"He's locked away in an insane asylum," Jackie stood up from the table.

"He was locked up Jackie, but it looks like he escaped. They found the body of a security guard at the asylum so they think Gordon's coming back for us again." Roger looked at Sarah with confusion in his eyes.

"Harry Gordon was put away three months ago. If he escaped why did the cops wait until now to break the news? He almost killed me the last time, and I go to sleep each night reliving it all in my nightmares. I don't want to go through that hell again," Jackie screamed, storming out of the kitchen, bounding up the stairs to the bedroom slamming the door.

She stood before the mirror, raised up her T-shirt staring at the scar across her stomach. Tears filled her eyes and without warning her eyes changed to bright red, her teeth became pointed as Stephanie appeared in a rage. She could feel Jackie's pain. She picked up the heavy mirror and fired it through the bedroom window with a loud shattering crash. She screamed and hissed, her mouth opens wide, her teeth like miniature daggers.

"Gordon will die for this, Jackie. I promise you he will die," Stephanie hissed. Jackie returned to hear the others outside pounding on the door.

She looked around and saw the shattered window. She couldn't remember anything. She walked to the door and unlocked it.

"Are you all right Jackie?" Ben asked as he came in and saw the broken window.

Roger and Sarah looked through the broken glass and saw the mirror below in a million pieces. The mirror was big and heavy and it took both Roger and Ben to bring it up the stairs. How the hell did Jackie manage to fire it through the window? Sarah looked back at Jackie and a little look of fear passed her face for an instant.

"I'm sorry; I lost control for a while. I guess I don't know my own strength," she tried to smile.

"Fuck!" Ben exclaimed with surprise in his voice looking at Jackie wondering where she got that incredible strength.

"Jackie, you had a nasty experience with Gordon the last time. I guess when Sarah said he was back, suppressed memories and rage got unleashed, and I don't blame you, remind me not to get on your bad side okay," Ben tried to make her feel better as he hugged her tight.

Outside Harry heard all the fuss and saw the mirror come flying through the window. He smiled, walking from his hiding place. It was time to strike, his eyes opened wide with rage, he came running from the woods kicking down the timber gate at the back of the house.

They were walking back to the kitchen when there were two loud bangs on the door. Jackie held Ben's hand so tight she almost crushed it.

"It's Gordon," Ben yelled as the door was kicked open and the menacing hulking figure of Harry Gordon stood grinning back at them.

"Honey, I'm home," he said with an evil laugh gripping the hatchet with both hands.

Ben tried to pull away from her grasp.

"Ben, no," She held him back.

"You're all going to die. This has been a long time, coming now feel the pain and scream," Harry yelled, running at Jackie swinging the axe wildly.

They all screamed as he thundered toward them. Ben pushed Jackie out of his way and Harry went crashing into him, sending him flying against the wall. Ben rebounded off the wall with a groan, the force of the impact winded him and he slid to the ground. Gordon grabbed him by the throat, picking him clean off the floor slamming him against the wall again. Ben tried to get to his feet.

"Ha! Not so tough now, are you, boy?" he growled at Ben pushing the axe handle across his throat, pinning him to the wall choking him.

Ben gasped for breath, trying to push Gordon away. Harry yelled pushing his arms skyward until Ben's feet dangled off the floor. Roger came from behind, smashing a kitchen chair across Gordon's back. Harry dropped Ben and turned around to face Roger who had run out the back door. Ben got to his feet and ran down the hallway, out the front door. He ran to the others around the back.

"Let's get the fuck out of here now," he yelled as they ran to the woods.

Harry walked behind them. He enjoyed seeing them running from him. He stopped when a cop car came to a screeching halt as the four ran out in front of it.

A cop got out, slamming the door.

"What the hell are you doing? You could have been killed," the officer looked sternly at them.

Jackie was out of breath and panting.

"Officer, you have to believe us when we tell you we're running from a psychopath named Harry Gordon. He was right behind us," she stopped as an axe whizzed through the air, hitting the cop in the head spraying blood across Sarah's face. She screamed as Gordon laughed and came running from the woods.

"Run," Roger screamed, grabbing Sarah by the hand.

They ran until they came to a steel works plant.

"Inside," Ben led the way.

Molten steel bubbled inside huge steel casks throwing sparks around the place. A factory worker came towards them holding out his arms to stop them going any further.

They looked at him with fear, backing away from him. Harry was standing behind the man with a knife held above his head.

"Look out," Jackie yelled the man spun around.

"Hello," Harry grinned driving the blade through the workers hard hat and into his head.

They ran deep into the factory as they turned a corner a huge furnace stood in front of them.

"If we can get him close enough, maybe we can throw him in and roast his ass," Ben yelled over the metal works.

Jackie walked away from them.

"Jackie, where are you going?" Ben yelled.

She ignored him. Stephanie was back, her eyes burned with rage, she stood behind Harry.

"Hey, dick-head, are you looking for me?" she asked looking away from him.

Harry turned around to face Jackie. She had her back to him now.

"Now you die bitch," he growled, walking towards her.

Stephanie laughed as his hand grabbed her shoulder. She turned around, her blood-red eyes stared at him and he was in shock, he swallowed hard

"What the Hell are you?" he growled letting her go.

She punched him, sending him flying against one of the steel casks. He lay on the ground in a daze. Stephanie screamed, her teeth glistening in the light of the sparks as she ran at Harry kicking him in the stomach lifting him two feet off the ground. He landed with a thump; she grabbed him by the collar, spun around throwing him screaming ten feet away from her.

He stood up and growled.

"I don't care what you are, you're going down bitch?" he barked walking towards her again.

Stephanie only laughed flying into the air, disappearing into the darkness. Harry's eyes looked everywhere for her but he couldn't see her? As he turned around, she swooped from the shadows knocking him off his feet again.

"I'm getting really pissed off with you bitch. Get your ass down here so I can kill you," he yelled as he stood.

Ben and the others could hear Gordon holler and they ran toward him. Stephanie came down behind Harry dragging him backward toward the furnace. She punched him twice sending him skating along the ground. He came to a stop at Ben's feet.

"Drag his ass back here now," he yelled as he and Roger grabbed Harry's arms and dragged him to the furnace.

Sarah picked up a pair of heavy fire proof gloves and a steel bar, opening the blast door. Flames erupted from the furnace; the heat was intense. Harry was in a daze, but when he felt the heat, he came around and struggled.

"No, I won't die," he screamed, tossing Ben and Roger across the floor getting to his feet. He stared at Sarah and grinned. Sarah screamed as he reached out to grab her. Stephanie came out of nowhere banging his head off the steel door again and again; she vanished before Sarah could see her.

Harry was dazed, blood covered his leather worn face, and he wobbled in front of the furnace, he was so dazed he didn't know where he was and he swung his huge fists wildly but hit nothing.

Ben came running at him screaming, kicking Harry in the stomach, pushing him back into the furnace, Gordon screamed as the flames engulfed him, he tried to climb out of the inferno. His fingers gripped the edge of the doorway and he was pulling himself out. Jackie was back, she slammed the door on his fingers, and he let go. She slammed it shut, and this time locked it tight.

Harry's screams echoed through the factory. His suffering was unreal, as he became a human fireball, the flames engulfing him. He waved his arms around banging on the heavy door, his flesh blackened and blistered before dropping to his knees falling forward face first.

Then there was silence. Ben, Jackie, Roger, and Sarah looked at each other, sweat dripping from their faces.

"Is he dead?" Sarah asked, hugging Roger.

"Nothing could survive that. He's gone forever and good riddance," Ben spat on the ground.

Jackie smiled, she felt alive and electric.

"Hey big boy you want to get me home and see to my sexual needs?" She whispered in his ear kissing him.

"How can I refuse an offer like that? Let's go home," he smiled.

Jackie looked back and her eyes changed to green as Stephanie appeared with a grin.

"I'll always protect you Jackie," she whispered before she went.

"I hope he's not like a Phoenix," Sarah said looking at Ben.

"Why's that?" he asked with a smile.

"Because he can stay in the fucking ashes," she said.

They all laughed, just as the cops arrived.

Inside the furnace, they could see nothing only a wall of fire. Suddenly, a huge hand black and burning reached out for the door. It clenched into a fist, dropping back to the ashes. Harry Gordon was the one that suffered because Hell hath no fury like a woman scorned.

# RISE OF THE FOUR

# TIME SAVERS

☩

Nothing much exciting happened after their confrontation with
the vampires and Harry Gordon over four months ago. Ben
and Jackie were getting along even better than before, and the
others noticed it. What they didn't know, was that after they killed the
vampire queen, her spirit possessed Jackie, and Stephanie was the one
responsible for their sudden spike on the passion meter.

They had been kissing on the sofa the last few minutes and Ben was
gasping for breath. He stopped kissing Jackie who was panting.

"Oh, don't stop baby. We're only getting started," she kissed him
again

"Easy tiger," he said with a smile.

She kissed his neck and stared at him with passion, running through
her veins. Ben stood up, stretching and yawning when suddenly; a
bright green glow appeared on the wall above the fireplace.

"What the hell," he looked in amazement as a piece of paper flew
from the light landing at his feet.

"What is it?" Roger asked, picking it off the floor.

"It looks like a letter. And look at the date, it says 2099." he looked
with disbelief at the paper he held in his hands.

"You're telling me that letter is from the future," Ben asked in awe
as Roger read over the writing.

"I think you better sit down and listen to this," Roger said as the
others sat beside Jackie.

Roger began to read.

"To whoever finds this note. We are in a time of immense peril, and
I fear the world as we know it has come to its bitter end. Nuclear war
has devastated the planet, and those of us that have survived this long
are dying off, one by one. The war has left millions dead and the
survivors, some humans have become marauding bloodthirsty
creatures mutated by the radiation. We are held up in a settlement

trapped by the terrible plague that remains locked outside our gates, but I fear our barricades will not take much more. During this year, of 2099, the world as we know it has ended, and only a few have survived. In our haste to protect ourselves and the world we love, we have sent this letter through a time portal to tell you there is a way to prevent this terrible conflict from occurring, in 2098, a young man became the second Messiah and set about bringing lasting peace to this world, but his evil brother wanted him assassinated, as he wanted this war to start so he could benefit from the sale of his weapons. In this letter, you will find co-ordinates to a place where a portal lies hidden. You will use this portal to travel to 2098 and make sure the survival of the man named "Christopher Messenger". Only he can prevent this war occurring by attending a peace summit, but his brother will stop at nothing to bring this war to its raging glory. I pray you will be successful in your mission. These may be the last words I ever write. God speed on your quest and my hopes and prayers go with you on your journey. John Moore, September 17th 2099."

Roger put down the letter looking at the others in shock.

"My God, what are we going to do?" Sarah looked at Ben.

Jackie stood up and spoke,

"If this letter came from 2099, and it's giving us directions to a time portal so we can go back to 2098 and prevent this war from happening, then I say we do it." she looked serious.

"I'm all up for it anyway," Ben stood with a smile.

"I will not miss this for anything. I'm in too," Roger grinned.

They looked at Sarah, who smiled back at them

"All right why not? If we can stop the war happening, then let's go do it," she added with a grin.

"All right, let's get the hell out of here and go time travelling," Ben picked up his car keys.

And another adventure was about to begin.

They were driving along with Roger giving the directions written on the note.

"Take a left here Ben," he pointed at a fork in the road.

"Time travelling, I'm feeling like Doctor Who," Ben smiled turning down a dirt road.

They drove for half an hour before Roger said, "Stop here. This is the place."

Ben brought the Mustang to a halt, and they got out.

"Where do we go now Rodge?" he asked lighting up a smoke.

"According to the directions, the portal should be located around here somewhere," Roger walked on ahead until he stopped at a huge tree.

The others came up behind him and stopped.

"Well?" Ben crushed out his cigarette.

"It's here. According to these directions, it should be right around here?" Roger looked around him.

Ben walked around a huge tree when a flashing green spiralling vortex appeared beneath his feet and he yelled "Holy shit," as he fell into it. The vortex closed in the blink of an eye.

The others came running around to him, but he was gone.

"Ben, where are you?" Jackie screamed, looking around her.

She stepped forward when the flashing green light appeared again and she stepped right into it.

Roger and Sarah saw the portal, they stood looking in amazement.

They looked at each other.

"Shall we?" Roger held Sarah's hand and in they jumped.

In what seemed like seconds, they travelled through space and time arriving at the other end of the portal in the year 2098. The world looked different to the one they'd left. They looked around them Jackie and Ben were sleeping by a tree.

"Wake up you two," Sarah barked, Ben opened his eyes.

"What took you two so long?" he asked, yawning as he stood.

"What do you mean, what took us so long? We arrived here a few seconds behind you."

Sarah was getting a little hot-headed now.

"We've been waiting here the past two hours for you two," Ben stopped and calmed himself.

"It's this time travel, what seemed like seconds to you was hours to us here. So, we're two hours ahead of our own time, back home. Now let's find this Messenger guy and make sure he lives," Ben walked on in front of them.

"How are we going to find him?" Jackie asked.

"The directions here say Messenger has his own commune close to here, like Jesus and his apostles." Roger concentrated hard on their location. Everything looked so different even though it was the same place they had left in the past.

"Walk this way, I think the commune is over here," Roger led the way and they walked for forty-five minutes until they came to what looked like a hippie commune.

"Oh damn, I forgot my Marijuana man," Ben said with a big smile.

The others laughed when a little car appeared behind the gates with three people. They got out of their vehicle walking to the padlocked gates.

"Are you folks lost?" a voice from behind startled them.

They turned around and faced a man so gentle like in his appearance, glowing with life dressed in a simple white robe. They felt so strange in his presence spiritually charged and invigorated.

"Please excuse our intrusion. We seek the one they call the second Messiah Mr. Christopher Messenger," Jackie spoke.

The man smiled a gentle smile and said, "You have found him my child. I'm Christopher Messenger." His dark blue eyes sparkled with heavenly enlightenment.

"Mr. Messenger we have travelled a great distance to meet and speak with you. I give you my word we mean no harm and what we have to tell you may come as a shock," Ben said, he felt humbled in this man's presence.

"You are all welcome here my children. Come, let us talk, and refresh ourselves. I do not think the side of the roadway is any place for a conversation." the man nodded his head at the others behind the gate they opened it.

They walked for a while, with Christopher explaining to them why he is called the second Messiah.

"I was fourteen years old when the hand of God reached down and touched me. I was walking home from school one day, when a bright, intense light enveloped me. While I was within, this divine light I felt an extraordinary power flow through me, and for what seemed like seconds, I received a remarkable gift. I knew the mysteries of the universe and everything became clear. I had to spread the word of God in a time of war and pestilence. It was as if I knew the pain of all the people around me and how I could ease their suffering. As I spread the word of God at age seventeen, I had my congregation of over two thousand people and it was then they called me the second Messiah and my destiny is to bring peace to this war-ravaged planet." he stopped and looked at the gang.

"You look worried Ben? Do not worry my son global peace is closer than you think. You fear that my evil brother will try to stop me." Christopher smiled.

"How do you know all this," Jackie asked in amazement.

"My dear Jackie, I know everything. You have travelled from your past to my present to protect me from being assassinated. A task you all accepted with courage and pure hearts. I promise you now, that if you can protect me until the peace talks in two days, world peace will become a reality," Christopher blessed each of them then went to his quarters to rest.

The gang sat around talking keeping a watch on Messenger's quarters.

"We have to be very careful. If this guy is the second Messiah, then there will be a second Judas," Ben walked around the commune scanning everything and everyone.

"But they all look so at peace Ben; how could you suspect anyone of them?" Jackie asked smiling at a woman in a white robe.

"The greatest trick the devil ever pulled was convincing the world he didn't exist. Everyone's a suspect Jackie and if his brother is that intent on killing Christopher, he could have the assassin here already," Ben's gaze connected with Jackie's.

The assassin was there, but it wasn't human.

As Ben and Jackie walked along with one follower, he told them of the evil brother.

"Joseph Messenger was a government scientist, and his speciality was designing weapons. His greed got the better of him, and he sold his inventions to other countries for massive amounts of money. Christopher was all that stood between him and his dreams of extreme fortune. He didn't care how they used his weapons or who bought them, if they had the money he would sell," the man told them.

Ben just looked at Jackie shaking his head in disbelief, then turned his head left, and right scanning everything.

Something wasn't feeling right, but he didn't know what it was. He was unsure of this guy, Messenger, and his followers, but he didn't know why. He crushed out his cigarette as a bell chimed.

It was now six in the evening, and Christopher emerged from his quarters to do his usual supper sermon. All his followers gathered at a huge table, bowing their heads. All except one, who was breathing heavy and fast? Ben kept his eyes on the young woman as she trembled and shook, froth dripping from her mouth.

Without warning, she screamed, leaping onto the table running towards Christopher. Driven by an uncontrollable want to kill, she had her target in sight. The crazed woman was within arm's reach of Christopher, when Ben jumped through the air, tackling her from the table. They both fell to the floor with the woman biting and punching at him. He rammed his fist into her face, knocking her off him. He got to his feet and stood over her. She was going crazy squirming on the ground spitting blood from her cut lip. Ben came down beside her and with a quick twist of her neck, she was dead. He stood and the followers looked at him with fear. He had just killed a woman.

"Christopher, she would have killed you," he tried to explain.

Christopher raised his hand to silence him.

"I know Ben, my brother is behind this. Please, my children, do not be afraid, He was protecting me from the evil I have spoken of so often. Thank you, Ben," he looked at the dead woman on the ground.

"Remove her body from here at once. I will pray for her soul later. Come, brothers and sisters let us feast and celebrate a victory over evil. For peace and the future," Christopher raised his glass and all his followers chanted.

They ate and drank their fill before it was time for bed.

"Christopher, after what happened here tonight, it would be best if we take turns to keep watch over you while you sleep," Roger said as the others walked with him back to his quarters.

"Well, my son. You have all done well here tonight and your reward will be great in the afterlife when God calls you to his kingdom. Good night my friends," he closed the door behind him.

There was only another day until the peace summit, but to Ben that day seemed like an eternity. Something deep inside him was telling him "Beware."

Roger sat in a chair outside the sleeping quarters thinking about all he witnessed. Ben came towards him with a concerned look on his face.

"How are you doing Rodge?"

"I'm fine only a little tired. We only have another day to go and we'll be going home. It's weird how that letter came to us of all the people in the world," Roger looked at Ben.

"Yeah, I've had the same thought myself. Why us? This whole thing makes little sense. Why would anyone want to start a war? Maybe it's for profit from selling weapons, God only knows. But this guy can stop it all by talking sense into their damn heads. But we have to keep him alive for the next twenty-four hours. Has anyone been to see him?" Ben asked lighting up a smoke.

"Nope, every thing's quiet for now." Roger looked behind him at the door.

"Ben, did you hear something?" he asked.

"I heard nothing!" he replied, throwing away his half-smoked cigarette.

Something moved inside the room.

"Ah shit. There's someone inside," Ben opened the door and looked inside. He saw Christopher sleeping, but under his bed, another crazed person was waiting to pounce. Ben tiptoed across the room, looked under the bed, but there was nothing there. He stood up and saw it bearing down on him from across the room. It growled, jumping on top of him. Christopher woke up to the two fighting on the floor.

Ben pounded its head off the ground and punched it with all he had, making blood squirt from its nose and mouth, he grabbed the crazies head from behind and with a roar snapped its neck. He was breathing heavy rising to face Christopher. This guy is hiding something and Ben wanted to know what it was.

"Why does your brother want you dead?" he barked.

Christopher said nothing.

"There's something you're not telling us, you son of a bitch. Now, talk!" Ben yelled pinning him to the wall.

Christopher grinned, then laughed an evil laugh and outside, the sound of moans echoed throughout the commune.

"My dear boy, how stupid you are. When you defeated Harry Gordon, I came back for my chainsaw and I told you I would return," Christopher's eyes burned red with evil.

Ben stepped back from him.

"Christopher Messenger my ass, I have to give you credit Satan, you even had me fooled until now," he clenched his fists as the devil revealed himself, his typical black clothing and those evil eyes.

"I told you I would return Ben," he grinned.

"And I told you we'll be waiting. Be it the past, present or future, we'll kick your ass back to hell," Ben screamed, the devil just laughed a deep evil laugh.

"I admire your courage my boy," he walked out the door to command his horde of demons.

Sarah and Jackie came running to their side.

"Ben what's going on?" Sarah asked.

"It's Satan. He tricked us all into coming here. It was all a lie. Now he will kill us," Ben looked at Jackie with surprise when he saw her eyes turn red with rage and her teeth become long and pointed.

"It is they who will die," Stephanie, hissed flying high into the air, swooping down screaming, her long claws severing heads from bodies.

"Fucking hell, it's Stephanie. How did she? Who cares? She's on our side now. Let's go kick some fucking ass, and I'm in one bad mood now boy," Ben yelled as the three of them joined Stephanie in the fight.

Stephanie's presence shocked Satan and he looked at her with rage in his eyes.

"No, No, this cannot be happening. It was to be my victory tonight," he yelled.

"Kill them my children, kill them all," he screamed disappearing in a cloud of smoke leaving his demons to fight it out.

Ben fought like an animal, breaking necks and smashing faces. Sarah was like an insane bitch kicking and punching at the demons. Roger got mad punching one in the mouth, knocking it to the ground where he kicked and stamped on its head until it burst into flames vanishing in a puff of smoke.

The sun was rising, and the demons screamed as the sun's rays broke over the hillside. Stephanie had to disappear back inside Jackie or she would die. One by one, the demons tried to run to escape the sun's rays, but they burst into flames and disappeared. The smell of death hung in the air as they looked at each other and laughed.

Ben looked at Jackie standing in the shadows of the buildings. He walked up to her and stared into her eyes.

"Stephanie, I know you're there, now show yourself," he scolded.

Jackie looked angry, a frown appeared on her forehead, and her eyes opened wide.

"Who's?" she was about to bark but went silent when Stephanie appeared.

"I'm here Ben. Don't be angry with me. I'm keeping Jackie safe and you. Being inside of Jackie is the only way I can be close to you, because you're the only man I've ever loved," her eyes practically glowing blue.

"Does she know you're there?" Ben asked, more relaxed.

"No, when I come out, she doesn't remember. I took care of Harry Gordon that day in the steel plant is that not proof enough I'm here to help Ben?" she asked looking for forgiveness.

"Now Stephanie, I'm telling you once and once only, okay? Do not come between me and Jackie that's all I'm asking. You're a valuable asset to this little team of ours and you can stay. But how are you going to feed? You can't make Jackie drink blood," he said with a disgusted look.

"When I'm in here with Jackie, I won't have to feed so relax. I'm just here to protect you both," she replied with a smile disappearing back inside of Jackie.

Jackie looked at Ben with a smile.

"So, are we going to go home or what?" she said kissing him.

Roger and Sarah just smiled, they all said it together.

"Let's go home," they walked back to the portal that brought them there and in they jumped.

They woke up back at Jackie's place as if they had dreamed it all.

"Is everyone all right?" Jackie asked, standing up from the sofa.

"We're all fine baby," Ben hugged her.

As he looked into her eyes, Stephanie appeared and kissed him.

"I love you," she whispered in his ear before she went again.

Ben looked at Roger and Sarah.

"Oh well it's still Jackie ain't it? We got a new weapon in the fight against evil now and evil better watch out," he laughed.

Satan was furious and was already planning his revenge.

"Damn you all. I'll make you all suffer yet, that I promise you. And you my dear daughter Stephanie will be the first to suffer," he growled, eyes burning red, vanishing in a cloud of smoke back to hell to begin his new plans.

# SCARECROWS

✠

O n an island somewhere in the Pacific, a bright light filled the sky. Fire burned in the distance, black smoke rising to the heavens. It was the remains of a cargo plane that got caught in a thunderstorm, lightning having struck one of its engines. The pilot shut down the damaged engine hoping that the good engine would take them the rest of the way, but disaster struck a final blow when lightning hit the plane again. It fell from the sky like a missile, diving nose first towards the ground. The pilot and Co-pilot tried their best to level their descent, but the plane ploughed into the ground. It skated along, knocking trees, ripping the wings from the fuselage, and glass shattered covering the two men in a hail of flying daggers. They screamed, raising their arms up to shield their faces, as it ripped through a small wooded area.

It came to a sudden stop. Inside the pilots lay slumped over the controls. A passenger lay motionless in the back. Karl Duffy, one pilot came around, though disoriented, he sat up unbuckling his seatbelt, and blood covered his face from a gash in his forehead. He wiped it off with his hand before he looked at the other man. He leaned over, placed his hand on his shoulder, shaking him.

"Hey Steve, are you okay?" he asked as the other man moaned and moved, sitting upright.

"Where the hell are we?" he asked unbuckling his seat belt. Smoke seeped into the cockpit and the two men coughed.

"We have to get out of here before this damn wreck explodes," Steve Howard was a veteran pilot. He was tall and strongly built. His appearance looked like Desperate Dan from those old Beano comics. He'd been flying planes for over thirty years and had flown this route dozens of times, but never had he seen this island nor was it on any aviation charts or maps. How could an island just grow out of nowhere?

Both pilots left the cockpit and searched for the passenger they had on board. They found him dead. Thrown violently forwards during the collision, he'd banged his head with such force it caved in the left side of his skull. The smoke grew thicker, flames, licking the inside of the plane.

"He's dead. There's nothing we can do now. Let's go," Steve cried as both men pushed open the cabin door jumping out. They ran to safety just as the plane exploded behind them with a thunderous bang. They were both thrown to the ground from the force of the explosion. As they stared at the burning wreck, rain poured from the sky

"Oh great, this just keeps getting better by the minute," Karl said. He stood up and helped Steve to his feet. Both men walked on, and after half a mile, they came to a stop at the edge of a long field. A light shone in the distance that looked like the porch light of a house.

"Let's go see if anyone's home?" Steve climbed over the timber fence beckoning Karl to follow. They walked on and stopped again. Karl was still bleeding; he wiped the blood from his face again. Lightning flashed lighting up the darkness, a look of horror appeared on each man's face. The whole field was full of scarecrows. There were hundreds and hundreds of them. Both men looked around them, trapped in a maze of scarecrows.

"Let's get out of here, this place gives me the creeps," Karl said with fear and panic in his voice.

"Come on. Calm down, they're just scarecrows lad. Let's go this way," Steve said, trying to stay calm.

Everywhere they went faces leered down on them mocking them, watching them. The two men didn't know it, but they were being watched. A scarecrow moved its head, looking at Karl and laughed an evil laugh. Steve pivoted around toward the sound, hard to tell where the laugh had come from, but seconds later; hundreds of voices laughed an evil laugh like a choir from hell. Scarecrows leapt from their perches one by one.

"RUN," Steve yelled at Karl.

The men were surrounded, everywhere they looked, and everywhere they ran evil beings blocked their escape. Every scarecrow was armed; Scythes, hedge clippers, knives, sickles and pitch forks.

Both men screamed as the scarecrows moved in. Karl fell first.

He screamed and kicked as he lay on the ground. Four scarecrows moved in pinning him down. He had a terrible look of fear in his eyes as another scarecrow came toward him with hedge clippers, blades apart. It knelt plunging the blades into Karl's stomach cutting him open. His screams echoed for miles around. Blood stained the ground as his insides were torn out. They stuffed him with straw and stitched him back up.

Steve watched in horror, fear filling his face. He had no time to even scream before they pinned him down. When the scarecrows had finished, they perched the two men up on the wooden crosses, then perched themselves back up. All was quiet. The two men opened their eyes as they returned to life. Their heads turned to look at each other. They laughed an evil laugh, and then there was silence. Two more scarecrows had been created.

*In the distance:*

Thunder roared and lightning streaked through the sky. Ben was sitting by the window in the airport lobby looking out. A fierce storm was brewing.

"It will be a rough flight," he turned to Jackie sitting beside him; Roger and Sarah sat opposite them talking amongst themselves.

On the horizon, black ominous clouds gathered, covering the whole area.

It was time for them to take a well-deserved break, from all the adventures they've had so far, and they needed no more stress or excitement just rest, fun and relaxation. They weren't alone on this trip. Joining them were their friends Mike Metcalfe and Nicole Williams.

Mike was a police officer. He had made more arrests than all of his fellow officers at his precinct. He was about five foot nine, with strawberry blond hair. He had Nicole's name tattooed on his left shoulder inside a big red heart. They had been sweethearts for over six years. Nicole was a language teacher, and she taught English, Spanish, and German in her adult evening classes. She was a tall woman, though shorter than Mike. Her teeth were snow-white and with her short black hair, they seemed luminous.

They all stood walking to the terminal gateway. Ben, Jackie, Sarah, Roger, Mike, and Nicole, each of them handing over their tickets, placed their luggage on the conveyor belt for a security check. When all was done, they proceeded down the gateway hall? They were greeted at the plane by a hostess who looked like a blonde version of Wonder Woman in her red and blue uniform. They handed her their tickets.

"Thank you. Enjoy your flight," she said with a smile.

"Thank you," Roger replied, taking their ticket stubs from her.

They quickly found their seats and buckled up. Ben and Jackie sat together, across Roger and Sarah, and to their front were Mike and Nicole. They had no sooner buckled up their seat belts, when the air hostess demonstrated how to use the life jackets, emergency oxygen masks and the crash position then soon after the plane's engines roared. There was a little beep from the intercom and the captain's voice came over the air

"Welcome aboard flight 367 bound for London Heathrow. Our flight time will be approximately five and a half hours and we will fly at an altitude of twenty thousand feet. Please fasten your seat belt. We hope you enjoy your flight and thank you for flying Virgin airways," and with a little beep there was silence.

The engines roared, and the plane taxied to the runway, picking up speed. The gang felt their ears pop as it lifted off.

"Shit! I really hate that," Ben dipped his fingers in his ears. Jackie laughed.

"We still have a bitch of a storm to get through yet. Better have those sick bags ready," Ben smiled.

"Just make sure you use the bags and not my lap okay," Jackie laughed. She rested her head on his shoulder and held his hand. An hour later, the others were asleep as Ben looked around.

"Don't expect me to sleep. If we're going down, I want the first parachute," he said.

"Oh yeah, and whatever happened to, women and children first?" Jackie asked.

"Or if we are going down, I'd drag you to the bathroom and give it to you good and hard, may as well go out with a bang Ha!" Ben replied with a cheeky grin.

"Oh, will you behave," Jackie giggled giving him a slap on the shoulder. She rested her head on his shoulder again and smiled.

"Go out with a bang. That's a nice thought," she whispered, holding his hand again. Ben was thinking to himself.

"Do we have to be crashing, fuck, I'd give it to her now if I could." The captain on the intercom interrupted his thoughts again.

"Ladies and gentlemen, we will experience some strong turbulence. Please keep your seat belt fastened as it will get a little rough for a while, thank you," the intercom went silent again.

The plane shook violently side-to-side up and down. Ben turned pale as airsickness set in. He was fine until he looked out the window and saw a bolt of lightning narrowly missing the plane. He grabbed a sick bag just in time and vomited hard. When he finished, he looked at Jackie.

"Fuck! I hate flying," he lay back in his seat.

Up in the cockpit things were getting serious.

"Damn this storm is getting worse," The navigator said, looking at the readout on his instruments. The captain was on the radio.

"Ground control this is flight 367. Do you read? Over," he listened for the reply. There was nothing but static.

"There's too much electrical interference coming from the storm. All I'm getting back is static," he turned to his co-pilot.

Without warning, a bolt of lightning struck the left engine tearing it from the wing in a hail of sparks and flames. The plane dove.

"Fuck! We lost an engine. We're going down," The co-pilot barked pulling back on the controls, a cold sweat on his brow.

"Mayday, Mayday. This is flight 367 we're going down. Repeat Mayday 367 we're in trouble," the captain stopped talking and switched on the distress signal.

For ten minutes, they struggled to keep the metal bird in the air, now they were going down fast. The captain looked in horror as the ocean rushed up to meet them. He pulled back hard on the controls. The plane levelled out skimming across the water.

"This is the captain. Prepare for a crash landing," it came out, loud and clear over the intercom.

Passengers screamed as panic and fear set in.

"Crash position," the hostess ordered and everyone bent forwards with their head in their lap and hands clasped behind their heads.

Ben looked at Jackie and held her hand; the plane shook and shuddered violently as it came down. With a mighty bang, they were all thrown forwards. People screamed as the tail end of the plane was completely torn away along with those sitting there. Flames appeared outside the rest of the plane, blowing like a flag in the wind. With a horrendous bang and a terrible sound of twisting, grinding metal, they came to a stop.

Roger was the first to recover. He looked at Sarah and gently shook her. She moaned opening her eyes. Blood dripped down her face from a nasty gash on her forehead. Ben was awake looking at Jackie, who seemed to be all right. "Not even a scratch," Stephanie protected her," he thought to himself.

They looked behind them at the other passengers, a jagged hole, twisted metal and flames was all that remained of the tail end. Panicked passengers screamed and cried. Some injuries were bad enough, that when they evacuated, they would have to be left behind. Badly broken bones were the main problem, and three people had both legs broken.

Bits of flying metal that broke loose from the craft as it crashed impaled seven people. The steel spikes stuck from two of their stomachs. One guy had been impaled through the neck, ear to ear; blood spurted from the wound like a water pistol. Two more were dead, both had metal pieces through their eyes. A little girl had a metal shard that penetrated under her jaw through the top of her head, alongside her, her mother lay dying blood pouring from her severed throat. Out of one hundred twenty passengers only twenty-five survived, the others including the captain and crew were dead.

Smoke filled the airplane and people coughed and gagged.

"We've got to get the hell off this plane before it blows sky-high and takes us with it," Mike stood up with Nicole.

"All right everybody off the plane now. Follow me," Mike ordered taking control of the situation.

They reached the emergency exit, but it was jammed. He tried with all his might to open it, but it wouldn't budge. Ben and Roger came in to help, and they pushed the door open. Flames surged into the plane, the injured passengers screaming as their end came near. Jackie looked back with tears in her eyes as they screamed for help.

"Jackie, there's nothing we can do for them. We have to go now," Ben caught her hand, and they slid down the escape slide, and then took off at speed into a run.

Twenty-five people ran for their lives as the plane exploded in a huge fireball throwing them to the ground. Pieces of debris lay scattered for miles. In a matter of seconds, it was over. Jackie looked at the burning wreck horrified.

"My God, those poor people," she cried.

"Hey, there was nothing we could do to save them Jackie," Ben hugged her. Just then, the rain poured down, thunder crashed, and the wind howled, the storm raging with all its fury.

The survivors moved away from the crash site. They saw a light in the distance.

"Hey, it looks like a house. Let's head for it," Mike said, climbing over the fence with the others right behind him.

They kept walking until they entered another field and their jaws opened wide with amazement. Scarecrows completely filled the entire area.

"What the hell is this?" Roger asked in a pissed off tone.

"Relax they're only scarecrows. Come on, let's keep moving," Mike looked at Ben with an angry look on his face. They moved on through the maze of scarecrows. Lightning flashed through the sky, lighting up the scarecrows making them look terrifying. Little did they know what was about to happen. One by one, the scarecrows came to life and followed them.

Ben felt uneasy as he always did when danger was close by. The maze of scarecrows seemed never- ending. No matter which way they went, evil faces stared down at them.

A woman survivor disappeared as a hideous hand clamped over her mouth pulling her back into the darkness. The others didn't even notice she was gone. Roger, Sarah, Ben, Jackie, Mike, and Nicole stayed together. A man's sudden scream ripped through the air. They all turned around to see the scarecrows tearing him apart.

"Jesus! Run, for God's sake, Run," Mike yelled as the fear and panic kicked in.

Ben held Jackie's hand as they ran and Stephanie appeared.

"Why? Does this shit always happen to us?" she asked with a vicious grin.

"Don't know Stephanie. It just does," Ben gritted his teeth.

She went again and Jackie returned. Twenty-five people got off the plane, but now only fifteen remained. One by one, the straw-stuffed demons hunted them down.

Three scarecrows jumped Ben. Jackie's eyes turned to red as Stephanie went on the attack, screaming as she ripped through the scarecrows sending pieces of them flying everywhere.

"Thanks Stephanie," Ben said with a big smile getting to his feet, unhurt, apart from a few scratches.

"You're welcome my love," she kissed him and went again.

While Stephanie helped Ben, the murderous fiends butchered five more survivors.

The house came into sight and the last ten people entered and slammed the door.

"We have to barricade the doors and windows. I don't know what the hell those things are, but they'll tear us apart if they get in," Mike piled furniture against the door while Ben and Roger tried to block up the windows.

Nicole was terrified and Sarah sat with her trying to keep her relaxed, but she trembled so much she couldn't stop. Roger looked out through a gap in the window barricade, coughing and spluttering on his bottled water when he saw the scarecrows like hells army, marching towards them in their hundreds.

"God almighty here they come," he yelled as Ben and Mike came to see.

"Holy fuck, what the hell are they?" Ben was getting angry now.

He looked behind and saw a doorway and some steps leading down to a cellar. He ran down the steps flicking on a light switch.

"If there's power there has to be a generator. And where there's a generator there's fuel," he said to himself looking around.

He found a big tank filled with gasoline, and on the ground were dozens of empty wine and milk bottles.

"Yes," he said with victory. He bounced back up the stairs the sound of the scarecrows pounding on the doors and windows greeted him.

"All right, now listen up. I need your help down in the cellar. There's a big tank of gasoline and dozens of empty wine and milk bottles. We're gonna make some Molotov cocktails and roast these bastards," he said as he turned going back down with the others behind him.

They filled the bottles with the fuel while Jackie and Sarah tore strips of cloth plugging it into the bottles to make a fuse. "That's just over fifty bombs Ben. Do you think it'll be enough?" Sarah put the last bottle in a crate.

"We won't be long finding out," he replied as he and Mike carried the last crate up the stairs to the bedrooms. He opened the window and looked down. There were hundreds of scarecrows as far as the eye could see.

"All right, make every one count," Ben took one from the crate and lit it. He threw it, and it shattered on the ground setting five scarecrows alight.

"Ha-ha! How do you like that?" he yelled with a grin.

For over an hour, it rained fire from the sky. They killed over two hundred scarecrows but they still kept coming.

"Damn, this is the last one," Roger said, tossing it out the window.

Down stairs, Nicole screamed. They ran to her, only to see a scarecrow had smashed through the window barricade and was climbing inside.

"Oh no, you don't," Ben said as he punched it in the head knocking it back. Quick as a flash, he boarded up the window again. The killers pounded the house with unrelenting persistence. An axe smashed through the door.

"Oh man, looks like we got another fight coming up," Roger said, looking at Ben who had a wide grin on his face.

"I know, and I must say a great start to the holiday this is turning out to be," he clenched his fists shaking his head as the door shuddered in its frame..

"Mike, take Nicole and the others into the cellar and stay there until this is over," Ben barked at the last of the survivors.

"Oh, yeah and who are you to give the orders around here?" A young man shoved his way through the crowd to stand in front of Ben. Several of the survivors turned to see the altercation.

"Listen to me little man, unless you can fight, get in the damn cellar before I kill you myself," Ben's eyes got wide with rage and the man ran down the steps locking the door behind him and the other survivors.

Just then, the front door gave way, and the scarecrows poured in like lemmings to the sea.

Ben looked at Jackie, Roger, and Sarah.

"You lot ready for this?" he looked in surprise at Stephanie, as she appeared to help.

"Oh! I'm ready," she hissed.

"Ha-ha, you always are," Ben led the attack.

Stephanie tore a scarecrow's head off with her pointed claws and ripped another one's stomach open, pulling the stuffing out of it. Sarah screamed as she swung a sickle slicing another one's head clean off. Roger had one on the ground and he stamped his foot on its head crushing it. Ben went mental. He ran at them tackling them to the ground, punching the ever-living shit out of them flinging straw parts behind him.

For the next hour, all that the survivors in the basement could hear were thumps on the floor as bodies fell every few seconds.

There was a never-ending procession of scarecrows. The more they killed the more straw stuffed goons appeared to take their place.

In the distance, the faint sound of a helicopter could be heard over the wails and screams of the scarecrows. The automatic distress signal reached the coast guard just before the plane exploded giving them enough time to triangulate the coordinates.

The gang heard the helicopter, but they kept fighting, forcing the brain-dead bags of straw outside, the burning remains of the scarecrows acted like a beacon letting the pilot know where they were. The helicopter flew overhead, and the pilot looked down and saw the scarecrows and the four fighting them. He radioed for immediate back up and within ten minutes, an army chopper landed and soldiers opened fire.

Scarecrows fell by the dozen. Ben, Roger, Sarah, and Jackie were delighted for help, and they called everyone up from the cellar.

The soldiers obliterated the scarecrows, threw their bodies into a pile, and soaked them with gasoline. Flames twenty-feet high streamed into the sky and everyone cheered. The coast guard chopper landed, and those who needed medical attention received it. Ben's knuckles were cut up, and he needed to have them seen too. The other passengers were in shock, but not hurt too bad.

The clean-up operation started immediately, and body bags lined the crash site as dawn approached. They all stood together watching them drag more bodies from the wreckage before they were escorted to waiting choppers to take them to a nearby Navy vessel.

The soldiers carried the dead to a waiting chopper and piled the body bags in. As they carried another body to the chopper, while their backs were turned, a scarecrow crept up to the site pulled a body from one bag, climbed in, and lay there motionless.

The soldiers carried it to the chopper that was now at its maximum carriage weight, piled the body in, and closed the sliding door.

The pilot started the engine and rotor blades turned. The chopper lifted off and flew toward the sea. Inside the chopper, the body bag opened, and the scarecrow sat up. It climbed out and then stood, knife ready in its hand. The straw demon crept up behind the pilot slit his throat from ear to ear. The chopper spun wildly in the air with no one left to take control it went down.

The soldiers on the island saw it ditch in the sea and before they could do anything hundreds of scarecrows surrounded them and their screams echoed for miles as they were torn apart.

This island of horror was not finished with our heroes yet, not by a long shot.

# THE DESERT MOON

It happened over a year ago, a military operation went disastrously and horribly wrong. He remembers it all, vividly as if it had only happened yesterday. His arms shuffle about in the way a sulking child would fold their arms and wave their body from side to side. This was no sulking child; he was in a straitjacket having convulsions as he told Dr. Samantha Anderson of a tale, only he lived to tell.

He was Major Thomas J. Sykes, a man in his mid-sixties, and well decorated for his service in the military, even receiving a medal for bravery in the Vietnam War. A trickle of sweat rolled down his forehead as he spoke.

Whatever he had witnessed, it scared him. He was still terrified of what was out there and he tried to tell as much as he could of the terrible events that took place on a secret army base a year prior.

"I was sitting at my desk finishing off my paperwork, when one of my soldiers, Private Eric Parker, came in. He told me the test site was ready, and the experiment was to begin in five minutes. I didn't know what was going on until I arrived. There was a laboratory situated at the base, and I was escorted through the dimly lit corridors to the test room.

I sat behind a thick glass panel where I could observe the operation. As the lights came on in the test zone, I saw two men and two women strapped onto what appeared to be operating tables. Seven scientists stood in the room with them; they wore face masks and protective clothing.

The tables tilted forward as they went from lying flat to a vertical position. The scientists inserted intravenous lines into each person and covered their eyes with black goggles. One scientist looked at me and then at the General who was sitting beside me. The General nodded his head for the experiment to go ahead. Above each of the test subjects were vials of blue liquid. I realized that this stuff, was the DNA from the damn alien we had captured some months before, was going to be injected into the subjects. The scientists left the room. A loud humming noise sounded, and the subjects screamed as the liquid was pumped into them. They struggled with their restraints each of them had a pained expression on their face.

The liquid quickly disappeared.

The people were breathing heavily as a blinding light filled the room. It was gamma radiation. I realized then that the liquid was a mutagen, and the radiation is what activated it. I was anxious as they screamed in extreme agony, but you could not see anything the light was so intense." He stopped talking; a deep frown marred his forehead.

"Please continue," Dr. Anderson, wrote in her journal, placing the Dictaphone recorder closer to Major Sykes.

The Major continued nervously.

"When the blinding light subsided, the room had gone dark. A deathly silence loomed in the air. The lights came back on and as the room became bright, I looked in and rose from my seat, my heart pounding with terror. The men and women were no longer there. They had been mutated into things so grotesque I can't begin to describe them. The General stood with a smile.

"This is the beginning of a new era for the Military Tom. Meet our new super soldiers, each one with the strength of twenty men, the speed of a cheetah, and a vicious streak like a hundred Tasmanian devils. Excellent work men," he said turning around to walk away. "Who were those people?" I asked with terror in my voice.

"Prisoners from death row, low life scum bags heading for the electric chair, rapists and murderers drug dealers that no one cared about or will even miss. They're more useful as guinea pigs in our experiments than dead slabs of meat. They're in the army now," the General walked off with a laugh.

The things were standing there, and they were huge, at least nine feet tall, razor-sharp teeth, and claws. They looked like something from a horror movie.

As the scientists and ten soldiers brought them out, all hell broke loose. What happened next still haunts me each night.

The door slid open, and the soldiers entered with their guns ready. The scientists followed. The monsters roared and snarled, rushing at them. The soldiers opened fire, but the monsters kept coming almost indestructible. I watched in horror, as the soldiers were torn apart, blood sprayed across the glass where I was. A scientist ran from the room sealing the door locking the others inside with these fucking things. The slaughter continued until there was nothing left of the ten soldiers or the scientists, but a massacred mess of limbs and blood. The creatures looked at me and pounded on the glass. I ran for my life as the nine-inch glass cracked. I was running down the corridor when I heard a loud bang and glass shattering, I knew they were loose and in the complex.

I pushed a button and sounded the alarm, but it was useless. Soldiers died left, right and centre. The bullets just seemed to bounce off the things they kept coming," He stopped talking, staring at the doctor who was documenting everything he was saying. She took a sip from her coffee mug looking at the man.

"Continue,"

He cleared his throat and swallowed.

"Outside the building, we had tanks and grenades ready. We stood there waiting, all we could hear were gunshots, and screams as the things came charging through the doorway into view. I gave the order to "open fire," and the thunder of the tank's guns rattled the ground. Grenades whizzed through the air exploding with a roaring bang. The men ceased fire. Dust covered the entire area, and we waited until it cleared, waiting to see four dead mutants. Nothing could have survived that, nothing. The dust settled, then we heard a growl from behind the cloud and they came hollering and screaming at us.

I heard the sound of a helicopter as the General was evacuated from the site. The rest of us were expendable assets. Two hundred men died that day. I ran for my life and hid myself beneath a tank and there I stayed for five long terrifying days until help finally arrived. And here

I am.

Operation Desert Moon was a failure. Dear God those things are still out there. Do you hear me they're still out there," the Major screamed, getting up from his chair?

Two male nurses pinned him down.

"Take him back to his room," Dr. Anderson ordered. The black-haired woman stood, placed a pen in her coat pocket and left the room.

The sound of her high-heeled shoes echoed down through the miserable grey hallways, fading slowly.

Dr. Anderson's Mercedes convertible was on the middle floor of the high-rise car park. She placed the key in the ignition and turned it. The tires screeched a little as she took a corner. She was rushing home to see her sister, whom she hadn't seen in over a year, not since her marriage to Ben. Roger and Sarah would be there too.

She drove for thirty minutes when her house came into view, and there parked in the driveway was Ben's Mustang. She stopped her car behind it, and four people walked to meet her. She switched off the engine getting out with a big smile on her face.

"Hey, Samantha how are you doing these days?" Jackie threw her arms around her and hugged her tight.

"I'm doing great Jackie. Work is going brilliantly and my mortgage is nearly paid off, so all in all I can't complain," she said letting go of Jackie.

"Hello Samantha, nice to see you again." Ben shook her hand, giving her a little kiss on the cheek.

"And it's nice to see you too Ben," she replied with a big smile.

Roger and Sarah hugged her and they all went inside the house.

The place was huge, done up brilliantly and looked very extravagant. The sitting room had dark royal blue carpeting, with paintings of birds of prey on the walls along with several bookcases that were filled with books on psychology, criminology, and forensic science.

They sat down on the black leather sofa and relaxed. Now, Samantha wasn't in the habit of talking about her work outside of her place of practice, but this case with Major Sykes was getting to her. She told them the story that the Major had told her, about the desert base and the experiments that took place there, and they could not believe it themselves. They were astonished and excited about this story and when Samantha had finished telling it, there were twenty-one questions flying from all of them at once.

Deep down, they all knew that behind every story, lies at least a small bit of truth, and if they had to, they would investigate this story with Samantha until an answer was found.

They looked at each other when Ben spoke.

"Do you have a recording of your interview with Major Sykes?" he asked cracking open a can of beer.

Samantha ran her fingers through her hair clasping her hands together behind her head before she slammed her palms on the desk and gave a little yell.

"Goddammit all, every time he tells the story, it's always the same. Not one-word changes. Fuck, I even believe it myself. He makes it sound so real. I'm a trained psychologist with a master's degree and I can't tell if he's lying or not." She finally calmed down and Jackie spoke up.

"Where we come from, you get to know what's real and what's not. We've been through things and seen things that you wouldn't believe, even if you heard it from your own sister. If we had ten dollars for every supernatural, paranormal, encounter we've had, we'd be rich. So, what I'm saying here Sam, is that, if this turns out to be real and Desert Moon really happened then you got the best ass kicking team in the world behind you," Jackie smiled looking at the others. Roger and Sarah were kissing on the sofa.

"Is there super glue on your lips or something? Every time we look, you two have your faces stuck together," Ben grinned finishing his Miller.

Sarah giggled a little, and then there was silence until Samantha spoke again.

"If I can get you into Harrington house, could you try to sort this one out because I can't, I just can't..." Samantha stormed to the kitchen.

"Jackie, you can tell Samantha that we'll sort this one out with her, and we don't care how long it takes," Ben winked.

Roger and Sarah stopped kissing looking at each other.

"Oh shit, so much for a relaxing vacation. He's an action and adrenaline junkie. He just can't sit still long enough to enjoy life," Roger shook his head at Ben, who was just standing there with a big smile.

Jackie went into the kitchen to talk to Samantha. She told her about how they would do their best to help her out and she was in good form for the rest of the evening until her cell phone rang. Samantha picked it up and pushed a button.

"Hello," she said in a low tone.

She listened to the person at the other end.

"Of course, I can come in. What's wrong?" She looked at the clock on her desk. It was a little after eleven.

Her face got mad, she grits her teeth, her eyebrows narrow turning her forehead into a deep frown, and she screamed.

"What do you mean Major Sykes is dead?" she listened to the reply.

"Cut his wrists, where the hell did, he get the blade? Look, never mind; get the cops down there now I'm on my way." She ended the call slamming the phone on the desk.

The gang looked at her in shock.

"Forget about talking to Major Sykes now," she shook her head in disgust.

"Come on, let's get to Harrington house and see what's really going on," Samantha grabbed her car keys.

It was raining hard and visibility on the road was very poor. Samantha was concentrating so hard that she didn't even notice the red and blue lights flashing behind her until the siren sounded.

"Oh shit." She pulled the car onto the hard shoulder and stopped.

The cop's car screeched to a halt in front of the Mercedes three cops got out with their pistols drawn, aimed at Samantha.

"Get out of the car now with your hands behind your head," one cop screamed as his thumb drew back the hammer of his pistol, getting ready to fire.

The doors of the Mercedes opened and the five occupants slowly got out putting their hands on the roof of the car. The cops ran over to them and bent their arms behind their backs, cuffing them. Another cop searched the car and yelled, "I have it."

He closed the door walking back to the others.

"Well, what do we have here? A blood-stained combat knife. It's looking bad for all of you. We got a tip from an anonymous caller saying that you were at the scene of a murder. A man named Major Thomas J. Sykes of Harrington house was killed and the culprit tried to make it look like he had committed suicide. Is it a coincidence now that this blood-stained knife is found in your vehicle?" the lean faced cop was in Ben's face now.

"Fuck, we've been set up." He coughed and gagged as the cop punched him in the stomach.

The cops called for backup, and their prisoners were bundled into the Police cars and taken in for questioning under suspicion of murder.

Ben sat in the interrogation room, his hands still cuffed behind his back, staring at the smouldering cigarette in the half-full ashtray. A trickle of blood flowed from the corner of his mouth as the lean faced cop looked down on him with his fist clenched to hit Ben again.

"Come on admit it, you lot killed Major Sykes and tried to escape. Don't give me that bullshit about being at Dr. Anderson's house when you received a call about the Major being killed. Now, tell me you little bastard or so help me, I'll," The cop stopped talking as Ben laughed.

"Get a life you ass hole. If we killed Sykes, then what reason could we possibly have for driving back to the crime scene? You pulled us over driving to the scene not away from it. If you don't believe me, then ask the others what happened." Ben's head snapped to the left as the cop hit him.

"You all planned your story so why should I believe anything you say," The cop shut up as the door flew open and the police chief stood there with the others behind him.

"Briggs, you have gone too far with your abusive behaviour this time. Release that man now." The tough bald-headed Kojak look-alike barked.

The cop reluctantly uncuffed Ben.

"I'll be seeing you again," he whispered in Ben's ear.

Ben spat blood on the ground, and gave the cop an angry look.

"If you weren't a cop, I'd lay you out cold where you stand," he growled in the man's face before turning away.

He walked to the others putting on his denim jacket lighting up a smoke.

"Are you okay Ben?" They asked. He nodded.

"You're free to go, and I apologize for the way you were treated, Dr. Anderson. We'll be in contact with you soon. Before you go, did Major Sykes tell you anything before his death?" The Chief asked with a serious look.

"He said nothing of any importance to the police," Samantha said, then walked away with the others.

The Chief walked back to the interrogation room where the cop that beat Ben sat on the edge of a desk arms folded across his chest.

"You incompetent fool. I sent you on a simple mission to kill Tom Sykes and frame Samantha Anderson. You couldn't even do that much right." he said with a cold look in his eyes. The other man stood to attention.

"I'm sorry General Sir, but they provided Dr. Anderson with an air tight story, and it was impossible to pin the blame on her." The man was trembling now.

"Pathetic fools; I'm surrounded by pathetic fools. Now you listen to me Corporal, you will team up with Sergeant Cole and follow them to Harrington House. I have a funny feeling our old friend Tom Sykes told her everything about Desert Moon and I want them silenced. Now go with Sergeant Cole and await your orders. Oh, and Corporal, if you fail this time, I'll have you executed. Do I make myself clear?"

"Sir, yes, Sir," the soldier replied he saluted and left the room.

Outside in the police garage, Samantha was talking to the others.

"Who would want to set us up for murder? And why would they want to kill Major Sykes?" she started the engine, put the car into reverse, and drove the five miles to Harrington House.

Another car followed them closely. The black man had a two-way radio, and he spoke. "This is Ghost Rider One. General they have arrived at Harrington House. What are your orders over?" he took his finger off the button and waited for a reply.

"Ghost Rider, stay with them, and don't let them out of your sight. When you get to the open road, kill them all and make it look like a terrible accident. Desert Moon must be re-opened. Those super soldiers must be found, and I don't want these people interfering. You have your orders, Sergeant; now go to it, over and out." The radio went silent and the two men waited.

Inside the asylum, Samantha and the others were in the morgue examining the body of the Major. Samantha looked hard at the wounds on the Major's arms.

"The cops are right Jackie. He didn't do this to himself; these cuts are way too deep to be self-inflicted. But who did it and why?" she released the dead man's arm.

"There has to be security cameras in the building. Maybe they'll give us something to go on," Ben left the morgue with the others in tow.

They went to the security office and watched the tape, hoping that it would show something, and it did.

At 10.45 pm, a man dressed in a janitor's uniform stopped outside the Majors' room. He put on a black pair of gloves and picked the lock. He pulled something from his belt and it shone in the dim light. Samantha zoomed in on the image and sure enough, it was the same knife the cops had found in her car.

"That's the guy. Now let's print this off and get back to the police and clear ourselves," Samantha said. She printed the image and tore it from the printer.

They never saw the two men sitting in the black Porsche across the way when they left the building.

The red Mercedes sped off down the driveway with the Porsche not too far behind them. For about twenty minutes, the Porsche stayed near the Mercedes when suddenly it sped up coming side to side with them. The passenger window glided down and the same man in the printed image extended his arm and fired his gun, not at the occupants but at the wheels. Samantha hit the brakes, and the Porsche flew by until the driver jammed on its brake, making steam rise from the tires as he turned the car around heading back for them.

Steam rose from the wheels of the Mercedes as it charged forward in a charge of desperation. The Porsche was on a head on collision course until at the last minute it broke to the right crashing into a tree. The Mercedes screeched to a stop.

"Fuck, is everyone all right?" Samantha asked as they got out.

Ben vomited hard when he got out, but got himself together and walked over to the crashed car pulling the driver's door open. The driver was gone, he must have scurried into the woods, but the other man was still alive and Ben pushed him back in the seat to get a better look at him.

"It's the same guy from the tape," he grinned.

"Now we'll get answers." Samantha was on her cell phone calling the police and within ten minutes, they were there.

Ben examined the Mercedes and there were seven bullet holes in it.

"You better come with us to fill out a report," a cop said to Ben, as he sat into the Mercedes and drove behind his partner in the squad car.

Down at the station they all watched the tape with the Chief.

"Well, looks like you're all off the hook. These men are Military intelligence and it looks like Major Sykes knew something they didn't want to get out, so they killed him. There's a high possibility you could be next and with those seven bullet holes in your vehicle I'd say I'm right. Now if you'll excuse me, I have a lot of paper work to do."

Something didn't seem right here.

The General went to the interrogation room, slamming the door his face red and angry. The two men were uncuffed, and they stood at attention.

"You fucking fools, let them live, and there's a good chance they know about Desert Moon and our super soldiers. Now we have to move faster than we had planned you morons. My army will be ready to move tonight. If they know about Desert Moon, then let's bring them along for the ride. You two take a small squad capture those people and bring them to our secret base. We leave for the Mojave Desert tonight. If you fuck up this time gentlemen, your lives will not be worth living. Now get out of my sight," the General screamed.

*Back at Samantha's place:*

They were all talking about the night's events. But little did they know the place had been bugged and their conversation was being picked up by the army.

"Major Sykes died because he had valuable information that could destroy the government, he told me and I told you. Desert Moon is real. My God those super soldiers are real," Samantha was saying when suddenly the windows shattered. Gas grenades exploded they all fell unconscious. Seven soldiers wearing gas masks broke through the door, dragging them outside to a waiting van.

The van sped off, and the soldiers removed their gas masks.

"We rendezvous with X-squad in thirty minutes and these fools will know all about Desert Moon," The same black guy said with an evil laugh looking at the five unconscious people bound and gagged in the back.

Four choppers waited at the base and the doors slid shut when everyone was on board.

"Good work Sergeant; it's time to finish this operation once and for all, pity about the prisoners. Beauty like this is so rare," the General said running his fingers through Jackie's hair.

He didn't notice Ben's eye watching everything, nobody touches his girl. He'd make sure this man paid when all was said and done.

His gaze shifted to four huge cages that were also on board. Whatever they were hunting, they were big, but he also knew things that big meant trouble.

# THE HUNTERS BECOME THE HUNTED

✝

Somewhere in Nevada, in the barren wasteland of the Mojave Desert, where the remains of a Military base stands, four choppers touched down. Sand blew all around. They were right alongside the building where it all started. The windows were all smashed, and the roof had been ripped to bits by the vicious sand storms that frequented the place. The chopper doors slid open, and the soldiers got out.

"Unload the equipment and set up camp double time platoon," a tall man named Sergeant Cole barked. He was a gun and ammunition expert and his boots shone bright in the desert sun.

They unloaded ammunition and artillery and stacked it in four mini- piles. The heat was intense the soldiers stripped to the waist their dog tags shining in the sun. Inside the building, the General and four armed soldiers checked it out from top to bottom.

"Be careful men these bastards are deadly and an attack can come from anywhere at any time, so stay alert," The Kojak look alike said taking off his desert cap wiping the sweat from his face. A soldier screamed firing his weapon.

"What the fuck?" The General ran to the room where they found a shaken soldier. "Goddammit private, what is the matter with you boy?" The General yelled in the young soldier's face.

The soldier pointed at the skeleton on the ground.

"Scared the fucking shit out of me, sir it fell right on top of me," he was trembling.

The others laughed, and the General screamed at one of them.

"What's so fucking funny Corporal? Do you think this is a holiday resort or something? Private Jones did the right thing opening fire. It could easily have been one of those things. You know something Corporal, you're a pansy, a bed wetting pansy. And if you don't get your fucking act together son, you'll be a fucking dead bed wetting pansy do you understand me," the General yelled.

"Yes, sir," the man replied.

"Look at this skeleton. Those things ate him alive. And that's what'll happen to all of you if you don't shape up right now. All right, get out of my sight you bunch of fucking lunatics," the General barked and the men left the room.

The General looked at the skeleton.

"Where are you vicious murdering bastards hiding," He whispered.

The tents were pitched side by side and a big marquee stood on its own, inside, the General made his plans. The same black guy Sergeant Cole came in and saluted.

"The prisoners have awakened sir," he said.

"Good bring them in," The General sat at his desk, his dark brown eyes squinted up in the light of the lantern above his head.

The canopy peeled back and the five prisoners were forced inside. Samantha fell to her knees and the Sergeant dragged her to her feet by the hair...

"Get your hands off her you bastard," Jackie screamed.

The General laughed, walking toward them. They were gobsmacked when they saw who he was, the so-called Chief of Police.

"That will be all Sergeant," he said as the other man saluted and left.

"Now, we all know why we're here, so let's cut the bullshit, and get down to business. I had Major Sykes killed; hoping that he hadn't told you anything, but sadly he told you everything. We want these things alive to train as our new frontier of warfare. Our new super soldiers will be a new era for the Military. If you are wondering how I know so much, I'm the one that helped to create them. And come dawn tomorrow, we will hunt them down and bring them back alive," the General laughed.

"You're out of your fucking mind. You saw what those things did to the last army group that were here, and now you will send those men after them on a suicidal mission," Samantha barked.

"A small price to pay for the fortunes of war my dear, soldiers die, that's life in the army," the General sat down behind the desk.

"Take the prisoners away," he said, five soldiers entered and removed the prisoners.

Unknowingly to anyone they were being watched from the shadows by the four creatures they came here to hunt down. Who was hunting whom?

Ben struggled with the ropes around his wrists cutting himself. Outside, the soldiers were getting ready for the hunt. They loaded Pump actions and rifles, mini rockets slid into bazookas and bullets clipped into magazines. Thirty men laughed and joked while they drank their beer. In the shadows, the monsters growled. They were waiting for their time to strike and when the time came, they would kill and devour all in a feast of terror.

That night the General slept until a shuffling sound woke him. On the canvas of his tent, the moonlight cast a monstrous shadow. Huge hands and claws slashed the canvas open to reveal a hideous monster. The General jumped to his feet, picking up his gun and firing. The thing kept coming; he emptied a full clip into it, but the creature's tough skin was like armour and the bullets bounced off it.

The soldiers slept on in their alcohol-induced sleep, hearing nothing. He put in a new clip of bullets and before he could fire, he screamed raising his arms to shield himself from the claws slashing through the air, slicing him open painting the canvas red with blood.

The soldiers woke the next morning to find the marquee torn to pieces. The Sergeant looked at the remains of the marquee and horror appeared on his face.

"What the fuck happened here," he looked inside. Blood painted the canvas, dripping to the floor. The Generals head looked up at him mouth still open in terror.

"Jesus Christ," he said as he ran from the tent.

The soldiers lined up as the Sergeant spoke.

"Last night the mother fuckers we hunt today came to this camp and killed the General. I am now taking command of this operation and the orders are now shoot to kill. Now get your gear, get out there, and kill these things," he yelled walking away into the campsite.

The soldiers moved out across the desert talking amongst themselves.

"Fuck this shit; I got better things to be doing than running around the desert after God knows what these things are. I should be in the Caribbean laying in the sun, smoking weed, and drinking Malibu," a black guy called Big Blue said putting a joint between his lips.

"Yeah, Big Blue got a point. Why does it have to be us out here after these things? They could kill us right now if they wanted to and I want to live a little longer than thirty-three," another soldier said fixing the red bandana around his head.

They walked on, with no choice but to follow their suicidal orders. Suddenly, a soldier screamed in agony. His arms stuck above the sand with blood soaking up through the grains like red oil.

Big Blue grabbed the man's arms and pulled with all his might, his huge muscles bulging, when the arms came away and he fell back on the sand holding the severed limbs. He threw them down in shock standing up.

"Bastards they got Rambo," he looked in horror at the severed arms.

"All right platoon move on and keep your eyes open," a soldier yelled and as he stepped forward, a huge hand came up from beneath the sand grabbing his leg. He screamed firing his weapon, but hit nothing. Two soldiers grabbed his arms just before he went under and they pulled with all they had. The man screamed as he came up caught in the monster's jaws. The men let him go and ran when they saw what they were hunting.

It disappeared beneath the sand with the body still in its jaws. The other three mutants were waiting for the frightened platoon of twenty-eight.

Two more soldiers went down, and then two more and ten minutes later two more. The rest of the soldiers were too frightened to move or even fire their weapons. Big blue skinned up a joint and stood there smoking, heavy sweat rolling down his forehead, staring at the sand moving and pulsating in front of him like it was alive and breathing. The monster jumped up grabbing him in its jaws head first and with one bite bit him screaming in half. It roared showing its bloodstained teeth and went back under the sand. Twenty-one of the thirty men remained.

"We have to get back to the base before we're all fucking killed," a private panicked running off.

"Jones get back--," a Corporal shouted, but it was too late they dragged the running man under the sand and the monster came up, standing there grinding its teeth. The other three appeared beside it.

"Open fire," the same soldier yelled and twenty guns blasted. The four monsters fell down and stayed there. The soldiers cheered as they ran over to see what the hell they had just killed. They surrounded one, kicking it to make sure it was dead. The monster didn't move. A soldier knelt down closer to see if it was breathing. "It's dead," he announced and stood to walk away. Behind his back it opened one eye, growling but it stayed still so did the others.

It took ten men to lift one, so they could only take two and the ten men were struggling under the weight, they had to leave two behind in the desert. The creatures watched them walk into the distance before they stood up and followed.

It was now getting dark, and the base came into view. The monsters were awake and starving now. The ten soldiers carrying one monster panicked when they felt it shift on its own. Before they could warn the others, it rolled off their arms and swung its claws severing limbs from body. The other soldiers met the same fate and the two creatures left behind came running from the darkness to feed.

Back at the base, the Sergeant was looking into the distance.

"They should have been back by now," He looked at his watch. He picked up the two-way radio.

"This is base to X-squad come in over," he waited for a reply.

There was nothing but static.

"Where can they be? They should have returned to base ages ago," he barked picking up a rifle walking to the chopper.

The monsters followed behind him and saw the five people inside. They growled and waited.

"What's the matter Sergeant getting scared?" Ben said with a grin.

"Shut the fuck up white boy. Just because my men haven't come back yet don't mean shit," he barked at Ben as he leapt from the chopper loading his weapon and closing the door.

He felt uneasy as he walked into the shadows as if he was being watched. He gazed into the night catching something moving around.

"Jones if that's you I'll kick your ass," he stopped, putting the rifle to his shoulder as something knocked over a barrel. He walked over to where the noise came from and looked down. Six huge footprints lead away from the area.

"Motherfucker," he said standing up, turning around.

A huge hand swallowed his face crushing his skull spraying his brains all over the place. He got off a single shot before the hand grabbed him, alerting the others in the chopper.

"Oh, fuck they're here. Samantha, you wanted to know if these things were real? well, here's your chance," Jackie said swallowing hard.

Roger and Sarah were quiet. Ben roared, breaking free from the ropes around his wrists and untied the others. "Let's get out in the open. It'll be safer than being trapped in here," he opened the door and stepped out.

They carefully moved away when Samantha yelled. They had found the Sergeant's body.

"Christ his head has been crushed to bits," she looked at the headless corpse.

The monsters were so close they could have reached and touched them.

"Remember what the Major said in his story. Guns, tanks, nothing could stop them so how the fuck do we stop them," Sarah looked at Jackie, who was too busy looking at the huge footprints. Roger and Sarah were talking amongst themselves about the events of the past few days and Ben was looking around when the monsters got hungry again and attacked. Jackie screamed as the hideous things came charging from the darkness.

"Run for cover," Ben yelled as he led the way into a building slamming the doors behind him.

The doors were blown to pieces as the monsters came crashing through them. The cellar door closed just in time as the creatures failed to see where they went catching the mutants off guard. A little light switched on and they all stood still. "Did you see the size of those things? They have to be at least nine feet tall," Roger whispered, catching his breath leaning against the wall.

"We must wait until they go to get out of here or they'll rip us apart if we try to run now," Sarah whispered.

The mutants moved around upstairs, and then suddenly, they stopped.

"These bastards are smart, make us think they're gone so we'll go up," Jackie hugged Ben.

Samantha was silent for the next six hours until fear got a hold of her. She screamed and ran up the stairs, pulling the door open. There was nothing there. The others were calling her back down. "Samantha, close the door and come back down," Roger said.

"They're gone now is our chance," she said.

Jackie walked toward her. Without warning, a huge hand caught Samantha dragging her screaming through the doorway.

"Samantha," Jackie yelled, running up the stairs with Ben beside her. They got there just in time to see Samantha ripped in two.

"No," Jackie screamed.

She looked at her sister and tried to run to her, Ben and Roger pulled her back just as the creature's claws flew past. She cried on his shoulder.

"Jackie, I'm sorry about Samantha. But what the hell was she thinking going up there?" he hugged her tight.

"One thing's for sure, those bastards will pay for this, I swear they will," she screamed.

For the next four hours, they huddled together waiting for their chance to get out.

Ben got to his feet and cautiously climbed the stairs with the others following close behind.

He glanced at his watch

"It's gone past seven in the morning, they should be gone by now," he replied opening the door with caution he peeped out. The coast seemed to be clear, nothing moved. He opened the door all the way and stepped out.

"It's all right they're gone. Let's move while we can," he called the others to join him.

They crept across the floor passing a pool of blood that lay by the wall. Tears burned Jackie's eyes as she relived the death of her sister again. They emerged into the daylight and looked around at the empty camp.

Just then, the monsters came back for more fun. They all ran back into the building and into the basement again, this time the mutants were more determined to get them and they pounded on the door trying to break it down. With every bang, the door shuddered and cracked giving way.

The four were silent when they heard the timber stairs creak and squeak as the mutant's footsteps came closer. They hid in the darkest corner they could find huddled together and dared not move. The mutants reached the end of the stairs looking around sniffing the air watching for any movement.

The gang waited. Sweat dripping from Jackie's face and her heart pounded hard in her chest. Ben gently squeezed her hand the monsters turned around and walked back up the stairs.

"Fucking hell that was close," Sarah whispered gasping for breath coming out of the shadows with Roger. He wiped the sweat from his eyes and looked at Jackie.

"Did you see the size of those things?" he said trembling.

"They know we're in here now. They couldn't see us this time, so they gave up, but I'm not staying around. Let's get the hell out of here, back to the chopper. If they corner us in here, it could be the end for us all," Ben took Jackie by the hand.

Night was falling, and the sky had turned to an orange red colour. A rat scurried along. It sniffed at the spot where the mutants had stood and ran squealing into the shadows. Four silhouettes moved toward the chopper and halted.

"Why did you stop?" Sarah hissed at Ben.

"Do you hear that?"

"I hear nothing," she looked around her.

"Exactly, it's too damn quiet," he said as they moved on again.

The chopper door slid open, and they climbed in.

"I wish I knew how to fly this thing," Jackie said gazing at the pilot's seat.

Suddenly, the chopper shuddered. They screamed and held on to each other, and before they knew what was going on, the chopper was flipped over on its side, and then sent skating along in a shower of sparks. They screamed as the chopper banged into a huge vat puncturing a hole in its side. The liquid poured out all over the chopper in a wave of corrosive death, anything it touched smoked and melted. If this stuff met flesh, the pain would be excruciating.

"Everybody out now," Ben yelled as he tried to open the door but it wouldn't budge. Roger helped him and the door gave way. The fumes from the liquid were building up and stinging their eyes. They opened the door tumbling to the ground gasping for breath. The monsters moved in for the kill.

"Jesus, where am I?" Roger said his eyes blood red and stinging.

"Damn that stuff has messed us up for now, we can't put up a fight in this state," Ben barked as they backed away from the things coming towards them.

The monsters attacked swinging their claws wildly. The gang ducked and weaved their way around them.

"Keep running there is no way to take these bastards out now," Sarah yelled as they ran into the desert with the things behind them. They followed for a while, but stopped and turned back.

After a while, the gang came to a cave where they huddled up and slept. When they woke up the sun was splitting the stones. They sat there silent until Roger came up with a plan.

"You remember the story Sykes told, that guns and tanks couldn't stop these things? Maybe they're like steel on the outside, but, what if we could pop a grenade down their throats, it might work," he armed the sweat from his face.

Ben smiled and stood with that sparkle in his eye again.

"Let's do it, we can take these bastards out and bring this nightmare to an end," he grinned.

They all agreed to fight, and they waited for the sun to go down before setting off on their terrifying mission.

The base came into sight and they looked at each other.

"Death to the bastards," Jackie screamed.

"Death to the bastards," they all yelled. They marched into the base like the lunatics they are, proud, strong, angry, and ready to kill.

The creatures came out of the sand roaring then disappeared back beneath it. The smell of death was in the air and this day only four will survive, but which four will it be?

"They will pay for what they have done to you, my sister. We will make them suffer," Jackie hissed as the wind blew dust around her feet.

# THE FINAL STAND

Jackie stood looking at the crescent moon, her thoughts on the death of her sister. In the distance, a coyote howled. She smiled a wry smile as she thought of killing the mutants and she walked back to the base. Ben loaded grenades into his pockets, excitement running through him as he thought of the action to come. Jackie was silent as she loaded grenades into her pockets.

"Let's go get these motherfuckers," she growled, taking command for the first time, the trap was set now the waiting game began.

All four monsters entered the base from behind, spreading out, hoping to catch the gang off guard. The final battle was about to begin. Ben and Roger hid behind a bunch of steel barrels and kept a sharp look out. Jackie and Sarah were about twenty feet in front, grenades at the ready. One mutant came into view and Jackie's eyes burned with rage. She held up a grenade pulling out the pin, waiting. It moved closer and opened its mouth to roar when Jackie stood up firing the grenade right into its mouth. It ran at her, but time ran out, the grenade exploded, blowing its head to bits, it disintegrated like a bowl of stew being slammed against a wall.

She laughed and ran over to the body.

"Get down," Sarah screamed as another one appeared behind her. She fell to the ground and Sarah threw a second grenade and bang another mutant bit the dust.

Ben and Roger were smiling as the girls laughed and danced until Roger saw something move beside them in the shadows. He tapped Ben on the shoulder, and pointed. Ben put his head over the barrels to get a closer look only to come face to face with the last two.

"Oh shit," he whimpered the mutants pulling him over the barrels.

It had Ben held off the ground and he kicked and punched until he remembered the grenades in his pockets. Roger was way ahead; he pulled the pin and threw it at the mutant. It caught the flying grenade with its free hand holding it in front of Ben. There were only three seconds left and Ben broke free from the monster's grasp leaping behind the barrels. There was an explosion; they looked up to see the creature split in half lying dead on the ground.

The last one stood behind Roger and another grenade whizzed through the air, landing at the monsters' feet, stupidly it bent over and picked it up holding it in front of its face looking at it inquisitively and was about to roar when the grenade exploded, blowing its arm and head clean off, the body dropped to the ground sending dust flying all around. Ben and Roger ran towards the girls as the last monster fell down dead.

"We did it," Jackie screamed, throwing her arms around Ben. They were not smiling for long. Suddenly, the ground shook and cracked open and more mutants rose from the desert sand surrounding them. "The bastards have reproduced," Ben yelled as he tumbled to the ground with seven mutants tearing into him. Jackie screamed as they closed in on her.

She woke up in a cold sweat panting heavy, and then looked at Ben fast asleep beside her she was in her sister's house unharmed.

"Fucking hell, what a nightmare," she lay back down cuddling up to Ben.

*Deep in the bowels of Hell:*
Satan paced back and forth across the floor in chamber an angry look upon his face.

"I have to destroy these four meddling insects before my plans of world conquest can begin and this time there can be no mistakes. They have been fortunate so far but their luck is about to run out," he smiled and opened his hand and, in his palm, a little flame danced and flickered, Satan walked to fiery pit filled with molten lava. He got down on one knee placing the little flame on the ground, it hopped and skipped across the floor jumping into the molten pit.

He got to his feet.

"My creature of flame will turn you to ash Ben, and you miserable interfering maggots will know what Hell feels like. You will know the agony of Hell-fire," he yelled and laughed raising his hand sky-ward flames erupting all around him.

# OTHER TITLES BY DAMON RAVENBLOOD

The Devil and the Awesome Four Vol. 1 Rise of the Four
The Devil and the Awesome Four Vol. II Resurrector

Coming in 2023
The Devil and the Awesome Four Volume III Forever Four


www.damonravenblood.com

Ingram Content Group UK Ltd.
Milton Keynes UK
UKHW010756150623
423495UK00016B/359